Laurence Housman, William Blake

Selections from the Writings of William Blake

Laurence Housman, William Blake

Selections from the Writings of William Blake

ISBN/EAN: 9783337279547

Printed in Europe, USA, Canada, Australia, Japan

Cover: Foto ©Andreas Hilbeck / pixelio.de

More available books at **www.hansebooks.com**

THE SONS OF GOD APPEARING BEFORE THE LORD.

SELECTIONS FROM THE WRITINGS

OF

WILLIAM BLAKE

WITH AN INTRODUCTORY ESSAY

By LAURENCE HOUSMAN

LONDON

KEGAN PAUL, TRENCH, TRÜBNER, & CO. LTD
MDCCCXCIII

CONTENTS.

v

SONGS OF EXPERIENCE (1794).

CONTENTS.

INTRODUCTION.

" ALL beauty," says Walt Whitman, "comes
from beautiful blood and a beautiful
brain." The note of mechanical work is that
it has no individuality ; the note of a work of
art is that it is full of it ; so, in measuring its
beauty, we are measuring some beauty of temperament in the individuality that is behind it ;
and it is by understanding this temperament
alone that we gain understanding of beauty, or
appreciate the working of that fictional element
which must separate things of art from things
of history. Therefore, when we come to the
study of a man's work, who has done things
which seem to us beautiful, we must be sure
that we understand the temperament which
was the cause of his art. Especially must we
do so when, as in the case of William Blake,
there is so much in the beauty of his art that
is strange and difficult to comprehend, something, too, less easy to name beauty, which
seems to obscure instead of reveal the value of
his personality.

William Blake was born in London on the
28th of November 1757, the second child in
what was afterwards a family of five.   His
father, a small tradesman, kept a hosiery shop
at 28 Broad Street, Golden Square, and pro-
vided his children with no more than the very
elementary education then required of middle-
class respectability.   Blake was therefore, it
must be remembered, from the circumstances
of his birth, an uncultured, self-taught man of
genius.   His mind received its training chiefly
through an unrestrained following of its own
inclination.   From early childhood he wrote,
and drew, and saw visions.   The first of these
visions that we hear of took place when, as
a small boy, he was rambling through Peck-
ham Rye.   On his return he told how he had
seen a tree full of angels, and gave his evidence so circumstantially that his father, taking
the matter seriously, prepared to give him a
thrashing, from which only his mother's en-
treaty saved him.

It seems probable that at this period drawing was the least advanced of his imaginative
faculties ; but at any rate it decided him for a
profession in life.   Though willing, however,
that he should follow his early inclinations in
the direction of art, his parents were unable,
after having sent him to study for three years
at a drawing-school in the Strand, to secure

for him anything beyond an apprenticeship, at the age of fourteen, to Basire, the engraver, to whom he was to remain bound till 1778.

Under Basire Blake made further progress in drawing, and acquired competence as an engraver on metal. He also became an intelligent haunter of sale-rooms, picking up engravings after certain of the Old Masters which the light fashion of the day regarded as rubbish. "From my earliest childhood," said Blake, "I saw and knew the difference between Raffaelle and Rubens;" and he meant that he valued only the former.

But at this period, between Blake's gradual training in art and his already poetic accomplishment, a distinction must be drawn. It is not known how early, but certainly before he was fourteen, Blake had shown a high lyric faculty, independent of any training. No childhood ever made a more lovely claim for the recognition of its early genius than Blake's, when it produced "How sweet I roamed" as a proof of its attainment; this, with three others equally perfect, and several others less flawless, but no less purely the result of genius, were all written before Blake was twenty, though not published till, with the help of friends, 1783, under the title of "Poetical Sketches." There were other poems written

at the same time, and published in the same
volume, of which no pleasant mention can be
made. Yet in the worst of them are to be
found lines such as these, sufficient cause for
grief that they may not be included at their
right place of sequence :—

" My lord was like a star in highest heaven,
   Drawn down to earth by spells and wickedness;
   My lord was like the opening eyes of Day,
   When western winds creep softly o'er the flowers.

   But he is darkened; like the summer's noon
   Clouded; fall'n like the stately tree, cut down;
   The breath of heaven dwelt among his leaves."

It will be possible later to touch upon some
of the causes for the large inequality of per-
formance which so often disconcerts us in
Blake's writings. This, at least, is evident,
that poems which it is best now to put bodily
away were produced side by side with others
whose serenity and grace will make them for
ever delightful, and that this was the outcome
of certain defects in his qualities as present in
youth as in old age.

In the year before these poems were published, Blake, having finished with Basire,
and passed through some further training at
the Academy Schools, began life on his own
account. With the full disapproval of his

father, who disliked the match from grounds
both of prudence and small-class prejudice,
he had married Catherine Boucher, the delightful soul who was to be from that time his
lifelong companion and most devoted wife.
Without education, without—one would **be**
tempted to say—imagination, she had a won-
derfully receptive intellect, and infinite **sym-**
pathy toward the strange spirit to which she
found herself mated. And while she had no
correcting sense or discernment of the imper-
fections which harmed his work, she was the
more able to surround him with an atmosphere of assent, which must have had a sooth-
ing effect on the impatient activities of his
mind. With her at his side, Blake showed
an adroit faculty for finding happiness in a
life that, never quite ceasing to be a struggle,
fell too much under those marring influences
of poverty which some people curiously think
to be conducive to a high state of efficiency
in the arts.

Besides his wife, Blake found one other
sympathetic and kindred spirit within his own
family circle—his younger brother Robert,
whom, in fact, he had begun to train to be
an artist and engraver like himself. An end
came to all such schemes, however, in the
early **death** of the younger brother, which
took place in the year 1787. At the moment

of death Blake saw his brother's soul ascend, "clapping its hands for joy;" then he himself, worn out by a fortnight of continuous watching, fell into a deep sleep, that lasted for three days and three nights. Fifteen years later, in the pages of the "Milton," we find a pathetic record of the affinity which existed between the two brothers: two pictures, the one a replica of the other, each representing a man struck by a falling star; the one is named "Robert," the other "William."

To communion with Robert's spirit after death is owing that discovery of a process by which Blake, hindered through poverty from publishing his books in the ordinary way, was able to engrave and print them with little cost, save that of time. The result was a singularly beautiful form of book decoration, where each page of writing and illustration, blended together, made a decorative whole.

In this way nearly all Blake's writings were produced—the "Songs of Innocence" in 1789, "The Marriage of Heaven and Hell" in 1790, the "Songs of Experience" in 1793, and the long series of "prophetic" books, from the "Visions of the Daughters of Albion" in 1793 to the "Milton" in 1804.

Throughout his life, engraving in one form or another remained Blake's chief means of subsistence. At times, when he became too much absorbed in the production of unmarketable poems, the cupboard would grow bare. Then Mrs. Blake, without waste of words, would lay an empty dish on the table for dinner, a quiet and sufficient reminder to him to resume the task-work which **seemed** always to be within his means to procure.

On a general view, Blake's life was one **of** singular monotony ; its variety, indeed, came from within. The sense of sameness disappears when one comes to regard the extraordinary vigour with which work after work was pushed to completion, and fresh dreams and imaginations evolved. Through all his poems, his paintings, his faculty for seeing visions, Blake showed that he possessed in exquisite quality that art of living which his own art may help us to learn. Any one unfamiliar with his history would hardly believe that the spirit of delight which springs up everywhere in his poems and pictures was the outcome of **a** life lived almost entirely in the heart of London ; yet the four years of his residence at Felpham, under the poet Hayley's patronage, were the only ones spent amid country surroundings.

Evidently during that short and sore period there was an attempt on the part of Hayley and others to reclaim him to the ways of this

world. He was flattered into painting minia-
tures and other things foreign to his genius,
till, finding himself unable to produce work
in the old happy elation of spirit, he returned
in trepidation to London, not without caus-
ing some offence to friends by his precipitate
action. "The Visions were angry with me
at Felpham" he would afterwards say ; and
under those circumstances he had no choice
but to go.

In 1809 appeared the designs to Blair's
"Grave," the only commercial success with
which Blake ever found himself connected ;
and his own share in it was, indeed, one more
of praise than profit.

As age approached, Blake's value to the
outside market became less, but his artistic
value became more. Not only did his last
years see the completion of his most perfect
series of designs—the illustrations to the Book
of Job, and the beginning of a yet greater, the
illustrations to Dante—but there gathered
round him now for the first time a group of
younger men, artists, who had eyes to see
that he was a greater man than themselves,
and were ready to accept his influence without those reservations which had always been
made by his contemporaries. There is this
most eloquent tribute to Blake's unconquer-
able practice of the joy of life that, before

the end of his day, the wisdom of youth
met him.

He hardly regarded death, when it came :
he seemed to let it pass over him. During
his last day on earth he lay singing songs
inspired by the moment, and died so peace-
fully that his wife, sitting by his side, did not
know when death had taken place. It was
on the evening of the 12th of August 1827.

The effect of Blake's work has been gradual ; only little by little have some phases of
its strength come to be recognised. For a
long time madness remained the first note of all
criticisms about him ; and those tales of him
were considered the most representative which
gave him the appearance of a spiritual buffoon.
Then the date at which his poems were written
was allowed to him as a stroke of genius : he
had anticipated Wordsworth, and recalled
Shakspeare ; yet it was considered a draw-
back that his work became at times the much
more characteristic expression of himself. But
now it is not his share in the message of other
men that keeps him among the classics ; it is
his own message that has begun to fascinate
us. And to a clear understanding of this, we
can only come by an understanding of the
temperament on which it was based.

In Blake's art there may be said to be a
threefold aspect, corresponding to three inte-

rests or tendencies of his mind; and to one at least of these tendencies is due much that repels some people from his work. To all who are at all familiar with his writings, it will occur, as is more graphically brought home to them in his paintings, that Blake did not strive only for effects of beauty—that again and again he sacrificed beauty for something further, which the curiosity of his intellect demanded. And this he did with results clearly distinct from what will presently have to be indicated as his bad work.

Nothing will give us better the formula of his art than Blake's description of a picture now lost, said by one who had seen it to be the very noblest of all his works. Its value to our present purpose would not have been lessened had its execution been a failure. Blake's own words about it have remained, and describe with singular distinctness that threefold tendency of thought which so largely affected and explains his art.

The title of the picture is "The Ancient Britons." In it are represented three types of the human body—nude, to express their complete character. These, against a background of war and fierce movement of flight, convey for all time the divided powers of the human faculty. It seems a subject great for the hand of Da Vinci, but with Blake the setting is Gothic.

These figures are the three who escaped in the last battle of King Arthur—the Strongest, the Beautifulest, and the Ugliest Man. And in a passage of singular charm of thought —charming in its singularity—Blake gives his ideals of Strength, of Beauty, and of Ugliness.

"The Beauty," he says, "proper for sublime art is lineaments, or forms and features that are capable of being the receptacles of intellect; accordingly the painter has given in his Beautiful Man his own ideas of intellectual Beauty. The face and limbs that deviate or alter least from infancy to old age are the face and limbs of greatest beauty and perfection."

Then, separating Ugliness altogether from imbecility or disease, as subjects unfit for art, he gives as his Ugly Man "one approaching to the beast in features and form, his forehead small, without frontals, his jaws large, his nose high on the ridge, and narrow his chest, and the stamina of his make comparatively little, and his joints and his extremities large, his eyes with scarce any whites, narrow and cunning, and everything tending towards what is truly ugly—the incapability of intellect."

The Strong Man is "a receptacle of wisdom, a sublime energiser; his features and limbs do not spindle out into length without strength, nor are they too large and unwieldy for his brain and bosom. Strength consists in accumulation of power to the principal seat, and from thence a regular graduation and subordination ; strength is compactness, not extent nor bulk.

" The Strong Man acts from conscious superiority, and marches on in fearless dependence on the divine decrees raging with the inspirations of a prophetic mind. The Beautiful man acts from duty and anxious solicitude for the fates of those for whom he combats. The Ugly Man acts from love of carnage, and delights in the savage barbarities of war, rushing with sportive precipitation into the very teeth of the affrighted enemy."

This remarkable passage does more entirely to convey his range and temperament than could result from a far more elaborate process of criticism. The thought, where it touches Beauty and Strength, has a strange Greek element in it, changed, of course, to something more emotional, more spiritual, and less reasonable than the older philosophy could express ; and yet related, in that it upholds Beauty as the most equable thing, and Strength as the most wise—lovely and tender distinctions.

But the point to which we are led is the accuracy with which these three principles are reflected in all Blake's work. Each one in

turn claims and sways his sympathy : Beauty
by the tenderness of its eternal youth ;
Strength by the courageous proportion of
its brain and bosom to its work ; Ugliness
by its combative qualities and sportive precipitation.   For each principle had a health
and vitality of its own, which gave size to its
existence ; and each one he followed up and
expressed in turn with a clamorous delight,
just because it had that health and that vitality.
So the distinguishing mark of Blake's ideal of
beauty is the innocence that deviates least
from childhood to old age ; of his strength,
the fearlessness of a conscious superiority ; of
his ugliness, a sportive precipitation into the
very teeth of an affrighted enemy.

Therefore, when it is told of his work that
it has simplicity and freshness, relating it to
this and to that of other poets to follow, much
is left and ignored which is more remarkable and characteristic of his work, because
singular to it ; and, indeed, it seems of far
less value to say of him he did something
which Wordsworth and others did after him,
than to say he did one thing which no other
man did.

Simplicity, tenderness, exuberance of thought
belong to others as well ; these he did not invent ; but he did invent the means by which
to convey a new mind into the world, whose

touch set free those gossamers of thought
which one less spiritual would have broken
in handling. He gave expression to the un-
reasoning dreams and fabulous delights that
perish for most of us in our childhood, and
gave us also, on the grounds of Berkeley's
philosophy, a reason for being reverent as
well as glad in retaining them. He main-
tained that the evidence of the senses could
not be the outside limit of argument, while
thought and aspiration were capable of a
further range ; and if behind death lay life and
spirit, then behind all vegetable appearances
lay a higher substance, which spirit, not sense,
might discern.

This he was able to express, for once, with
sober brevity, in his disproof of " Natural
Religion," where the only warning the reader
may require is that he see clearly the two uses
made of the word " perception," which is at one
time applied only to the senses, at another
extended to the operation of the imaginative
reason. Much of the later hurtling prophecies
is but Blake's method of defending ground
less open to attack than he had calmness to
perceive. His further claim, that as accurately
as the senses can perceive matter, even so
accurately can the spirit discern the things of
the spirit, was no illogical descent ; and the
power and audacity with which he claimed for

the spirit to be judge of its own spiritual state, are before us in that passage of "The Marriage of Heaven and Hell," where he demonstrates to the Angel that one man's hell may be another man's heaven, and the Bible itself, under proper spiritual conditions, be turned to a deep black pit. This and other "notable fancies" Blake used in the likeness of thunderbolts, when forced into Protestantism on behalf of his artistic gospel; but he carried his Protestantism, characteristically enough, further than there was any real need.

Here was his warfare, with much of that "sportive precipitation" in it to which reference has been made, not to be compared for excellence with his peace. And it is in his peace that we shall best find him now : there, with eyes that could not see death, he saw a world full of small spiritual intimates ; every flower broke into acquaintanceship for him, every living thing found a new acceptance at his hands. He had a mind decorative of life ; a craving to quicken the expression of beauty and vitality that to his mind fell short under the conditions of nature. Following this instinct, his figurative touch fell on invisible as on visible things, as witness that passage in the "Milton" where he makes Time the city of a king, its ages moats and bridges, each year an invulnerable barrier, each month a silver-

paved terrace, every day and night a wall of
brass with gates of adamant, and every minute
an azure tent with silken veils. There is in
such stately imagery an exuberance of colour
rarely surpassed even in Solomon's more ex-
cellent " Song of Songs."

Blake's use of Nature was wholly imaginative, as was his use of gold in his art, as a word
in his poems, or as a colour in his pictures.
For gold, as seen and valued by the world,
was of all things the one which most filled him
with terror and loathing ; but, turned by his
hands from its base uses, it became the essen-
tial colour for things lovely and of good re-
port ; it fell in his threads of sunlight ; it lay in
dew on the fleeces of his sheep, and the wings
of his angels were covered with it ; it is the
colour left by the finger of God on a child's
brain, the note of compassion in a lion's eyes,
and the radiance of his great mane. This is
but one instance where matter in its literal
sense may be happily compared with Blake's
transforming use of it ; for in this differential
use of material things he always proved
himself consistent, nor had they any aspect
of interest for him till out of them came
spirit.

All this was the immediate outcome of that
temperament which it has been my main wish
to point to. And the result is no small one if,

keeping this as the object of our search, we become more able to detect, in moments when it is least marred, the spirit of delight which was his peculiar creation—a spirit which revelled not only in the charm of childhood and pastoral fancy, but in all things big with life, whether it were the lust of the goat or the roaring of lions—a spirit which found rapture and the fulfilling of a strange desire in terror and the sense of ambush, advancing with a fantastic fearlessness of tread up to the point of its adventure, and, at the very shriek of its recoil, finding ecstasy in sensations that matched the emotional force of its own life.

But it is impossible to say all the truth about Blake without something of dispraise. However glad one may be to find all words of praise inadequate to his deserts, there is in him, more than in most men, that other side to be considered, about which sad words must predominate.

At the time when Gilchrist's " Life of Blake," and much of the literature that centres round it, were written, Blake was to the general mind an unknown quantity, or, so far as he was known, an exasperating quantity ; and there remains a certain excuse, along with the gratitude that is owed to writers of that date, that they saw fit at times to write in an extenuating

and cajoling manner of Blake's bad perform-
ances and occasional bad manners. But the
effect has been singularly unfortunate. An air
of lenient superiority finds its way into their
reading of his strange but high intellect ; and
" our good Blake " receives a sort of domestic
fondling which is not seemly done in public
over a man of his greatness. To use a protest
that is Blake's in phrase—" the outlines become blurred," and the perfectly legitimate
and expressive exuberances of his method
lose their fine distinction under a general
atmosphere of allowances made for what was
bad work.

Unless we have the courage of an opinion,
which every one who knows in what he is really
fine must hold, that Blake did produce much bad
work, we are not likely to find either his greatness or his value. That there were personal
peculiarities, that there were limitations in the
way his gifts came to him, which rendered his
work liable to flaws, should be granted ; but I
think now of ill things more actively done. To
use soft words over the arrogance with which
he abused his lyric gift, and in contempt of
form wasted the field of his imagination, is to
endanger the separation which ought to stand
between his true work, which was expressive,
and his false work, which was without expression. And if such words offend, let it be asked

where does any sweetness or strength or clean
fury of temperament shine through those back-
eddies of so-called prophecy with which Blake
darkens counsel. Wherever it does, it is in
some recall of lyric thought, where prophecy
is relinquished, and the decorative hand with
its sense of gold restored. It matters little
whether the meaning can ever be wrung out
that is there; the process must always be
unlovely, and partial and artificial in its results. We may be assured that there is
nothing behind these bad mental manners to
give us a greater view of him than we have
for strength in " The Marriage of Heaven and
Hell," for sweetness in the lyrics.

The prophetic books have seemed, therefore, too large and too sad a ground to be
searched for any sound result, save where at
times some sustained melody of phrase carries
with it sufficient meaning to make it separable
from the rest. They are the sign chiefly of a
beautiful nature wasted for lack of equipment
in formulating disputatiously what grew out
of his better work, with all the thoughtlessness
and glory of a flower.

That Blake was not wholly ignorant of his
sins against form may be gathered from a per-
verse statement made in the preface to the
" Jerusalem," where he goes out of the way to
defend as metre a division of lines which had

only a decorative use. " When this verse was first dictated to me, I considered a monotonous cadence, like that used by Milton, Shakspeare, and all writers of English blank verse, derived from the modern bondage of rhyming, to be a necessary and indispensable part of the verse. But I soon found that, in the mouth of a true orator, such monotony was not only awkward, but as much a bondage as rhyme itself. I, therefore, have produced a variety in every line, both in cadence and number of syllables. Every word and every letter is studied, and put into its place. The terrific numbers are reserved for the terrific parts, the mild and gentle for the mild and gentle parts, and the prosaic for inferior parts : all are necessary to each other."

Mockery of contemporary opinion had perhaps a share in this expression of belief in a thing which he knew not to be true ; but it is an instance of what has already been called Blake's mental bad manners — a peculiarly harassing instance, since it binds every faithful editor to reprint his prophetic writings in the bad metrical form he claims for them, and not as the poetical prose they really are. All that can be said therefore on behalf of the fine passages from the " Daughters of Albion " and the " Milton," included in these selections, is that only when read with disregard to the

divisions of metre can their exceeding beauty
be heard.

Of those structural blemishes which are to
be found in so many of Blake's lyrics, the ex-
planation may be that he was a man of few
second thoughts. In his work, more than in
most men's, there is the impression of involun-
tary power ; and I have been told by those
who have seen much of the original manu-
scripts, that his poems as published are almost
always verbally the same as the uncorrected
draughts. It was in accordance, therefore, with
the undeliberate nature of his mind that there
should be a lack of the critical faculty for re-
vision ; it was to be looked for that this lack
should be more apparent in one of his imperfect education. And though there must be
regret that, through the lack perhaps of so
accidental a thing as culture in its exoteric
sense, he fell short of being our most lyric
poet, it is a regret that should not pass into
personal blame.

Through incompleteness his rare temperament was still adequately expressed ; and
though a little marred by nature, and a little
marred by man, he is a proof of the abiding
word of his own gospel, that "the soul of sweet
delight can never be defiled."

Of the mass of writings that remained in
manuscript during Blake's life, much was put

in order and published by Rossetti when he undertook to compile the second volume of the "Life," left unfinished on the death of Mr. Gilchrist; and to that source many of the later poems and prose extracts in this selection are owing. But a little still remains that has not seen the light, and has yet some claim to be considered new ground for the student of Blake.

A very interesting and unique example of Blake's style as a writer of narrative exists in a manuscript entitled, "An Island in the Moon," now in the possession of Mr. C. Fairfax Murray. It is too impossible to print as a whole, Blake's high spirits here, as always, having carried him into indiscretions of speech, not permissible in the print of modern days. But the extract of three chapters out of the entire nine, which I have been able to make, is sufficient to convey an adequate impression, and to give a pleasing idea of the spirit of banter in which the whole is conceived. It may be described as a voluble display of congested wits, where contrary minds come to loggerheads and final deadlock. Its early date is fixed by the fact that it contains the first draught of three of the "Songs of Innocence": "Holy Thursday," "The Nurse's Song," and "The Little Boy Lost." In inserting so much of this amusing trifle, my wish has been to give point to these selections as the expression rather of the variety of Blake's mind than of an individual appreciation. For the opportunity of doing so, my thanks are due to Mr. Murray, the owner of the original.

LAURENCE HOUSMAN.

POETICAL SKETCHES.

1783.

A

TO SPRING.

O THOU with dewy locks, who lookest
    down
Through the clear windows of the morning,
    turn
Thine angel eyes upon our western isle,
Which in full choir hails thy approach, O
    Spring !

The hills tell each other, and the listening
Valleys **hear ; all our** longing eyes are turned
Up to thy bright pavilions : issue forth,
And let thy holy feet visit our clime !

Come o'er the eastern hills, and let our winds
Kiss thy perfumed garments **; let** us taste
Thy morn and evening breath ; scatter thy
        pearls
Upon our lovesick land that mourns for thee.

Oh, deck her forth with thy fair fingers ; pour
Thy soft kisses on her bosom ; and put
Thy golden **crown** upon her languished head,
Whose modest tresses were bound up for thee !

TO SUMMER.

O THOU who passest through our valleys in
　　Thy strength, curb thy fierce steeds, allay
　　　　the heat
That flames from their large nostrils !　Thou,
　　O Summer,
Oft pitchedst here thy golden tent, and oft
Beneath our oaks hast slept, while we beheld
With joy thy ruddy limbs and flourishing hair.

Beneath our thickest shades we oft have heard
Thy voice, when Noon upon his fervid car
Rode o'er the deep of heaven.　Beside our
　　springs
Sit down, and in our mossy valleys, on
Some bank beside a river clear, throw thy
Silk draperies off, and rush into the stream !
Our valleys love the Summer in his pride.

Our bards are famed who strike the silver wire:
Our youth are bolder than the southern swains:
Our maidens fairer in the sprightly dance :
We lack not songs, nor instruments of joy,
Nor echoes sweet, nor waters clear as heaven,
Nor laurel wreaths against the sultry heat.

TO AUTUMN.

O AUTUMN, laden with fruit, and stained
　　With the blood of the grape, pass not,
　　　　but sit
Beneath my shady roof, there thou mayst rest,
And tune thy jolly voice to my fresh pipe,
And all the daughters of the year shall dance !
Sing now the lusty song of fruits and flowers.

" The narrow bud opens her beauties to
The sun, and love runs in her thrilling veins ;
Blossoms hang round the brows of morning,
　　and
Flourish down the bright cheek of modest eve,
Till clustering Summer breaks forth into
　　singing,
And feathered clouds strew flowers round her
　　head.

" The spirits of the air live on the smells
Of fruit ; and joy, with pinions light, roves
　　round
The gardens, or sits singing in the trees."
Thus sang the jolly Autumn as he sat ;
Then rose, girded himself, and o'er the bleak
Hills fled from our sight ; but left his golden
　　load.

TO WINTER.

O WINTER ! bar thine adamantine doors :
   The north is thine ; there hast thou built
      thy dark
Deep-founded habitation. Shake not thy roofs,
Nor bend thy pillars with thine iron car.

He hears me not, but o'er the yawning deep
Rides heavy ; his storms are unchained,
      sheathed
In ribbed steel ; I dare not lift mine eyes ;
For he hath reared his sceptre o'er the world.

Lo ! now the direful monster, whose skin clings
To his strong bones, strides o'er the groaning
      rocks :
He withers all in silence, and in his hand
Unclothes the earth, and freezes up frail life.

He takes his seat upon the cliffs, the mariner
Cries in vain.   Poor little wretch, that deal'st
With storms, till heaven smiles, and the
      monster
Is driven yelling to his caves beneath Mount
      Hecla.

TO THE EVENING STAR.

THOU fair-haired Angel of the Evening,
    Now, whilst the sun rests on the moun-
      tains, light
Thy bright torch of love—thy radiant crown
Put on, and smile upon our evening bed!
Smile on our loves; and, while thou drawest the
Blue curtains of the sky, scatter thy silver dew
On every flower that shuts its sweet eyes
In timely sleep. Let thy west wind sleep on
The lake; speak silence with thy glimmering
    eyes,
And **wash** the dusk with **silver.** **Soon, full**
    soon,
Dost thou withdraw; then the **wolf** rages wide,
And the lion glares through the dun forest.
The fleeces of our flocks are covered with
Thy sacred dew: protect them with thine
    influence!

SONG.

HOW sweet I roamed from field to field,
    And tasted all the summer's pride,
Till I the Prince of Love beheld
    Who in the sunny beams did glide.

He showed me lilies for my hair,
    And blushing roses for my brow :
He led me through his gardens fair
    Where all his golden pleasures grow.

With sweet May-dews my wings were wet,
    And Phœbus fired my vocal rage ;
He caught me in his silken net,
    And shut me in his golden cage.

He loves to sit and hear me sing,
    Then laughing, sports and plays with me ;
Then stretches out my golden wing,
    And mocks my loss of liberty.

SONG.

MY silks and fine array,
        My smiles and languished air,
By love are driven away ;
    And mournful lean Despair
Brings me yew to deck my grave :
Such end true lovers have.

His face is fair as heaven
    When springing buds unfold ;
Oh, why to him was't given,
    Whose heart is wintry cold ?
His breast is love's all-worshipped tomb,
Where all love's pilgrims come.

SONG.

Bring me **an axe and spade,**
　Bring me a winding-sheet ;
When I my grave have made,
　Let winds and tempests beat :
Then down I'll lie, **as** cold as clay.
True love doth pass away !

SONG.

L OVE and harmony combine,
　　And around our souls entwine,
While thy branches mix with mine,
And our roots together join.

Joys upon our branches **sit,**
Chirping loud and singing sweet ;
Like gentle streams beneath our feet,
Innocence and virtue meet.

Thou the golden fruit dost bear,
I am clad in flowers fair ;
Thy sweet boughs perfume the air,
And the turtle buildeth there.

There she sits and feeds her young,
Sweet I hear her mournful song ;
And thy lovely leaves among
There is Love ; I hear his tongue.

There his charming nest doth lay,
There he sleeps the night away ;
There he sports along the day,
And doth among our branches play.

SONG.

I LOVE the jocund dance,
  The softly breathing song,
Where innocent eyes do glance,
  And where lisps the maiden's tongue.

I love the laughing vale,
  I love the echoing hill,
Where mirth does never fail,
  And the jolly swain laughs his fill.

I love the pleasant cot,
  I love the innocent bower
Where white and brown is our lot,
  Or fruit in the mid-day hour.

I love the oaken seat
  Beneath the oaken tree,
Where all the old villagers meet,
  And laugh our sports to see.

I love our neighbours all,—
  But, Kitty, I better love thee ;
And love them I ever shall,
  But thou art all to me.

SONG.

MEMORY, hither come,
　　And tune your merry notes :
And, while upon the wind
　Your music floats,
I'll pore upon the stream
Where sighing lovers dream,
And fish for fancies as they pass
Within the watery glass.

I'll drink of the clear stream,
　And hear the linnet's song,
And there I'll lie and dream
　The day along :
And, when night comes, I'll go
To places fit for woe,
Walking along the darkened valley
With silent Melancholy.

MAD SONG.

THE wild winds weep,
　And the night is a-cold ;
Come hither, Sleep,
　And my griefs enfold ! . . .

But lo ! the morning peeps
Over the eastern steeps,
And the rustling birds * of dawn
The earth do scorn.

Lo ! to the vault
   Of paved heaven,
With sorrow fraught,
   My notes are driven :
They strike the ear of night,
   Make weep the eyes of day ;
They make mad the roaring winds,
   And with tempests play.

Like a fiend in a cloud,
   With howling woe
After night I do crowd
   And with night will go ;
I turn my back to the east
From whence comforts have increased ;
For light doth seize my brain
With frantic pain.

---

* Printed "beds" in the original edition.

SONG.

F RESH from the dewy hill the merry year
    Smiles on my head, and mounts his
      flaming car;
Round my young brows the laurel wreathes a
    shade,
And rising glories beam around my head.

My feet are winged, while o'er the dewy lawn
I meet my maiden risen like the morn.
Oh, bless those holy feet, like angels' feet;
Oh, bless those limbs, beaming with heavenly
    light !

Like as an angel glittering in the sky
In times of innocence and holy joy;
The joyful shepherd stops his grateful song
To hear the music of an angel's tongue.

So, when she speaks, the voice of Heaven I
    hear;
So, when we walk, nothing impure comes near;
Each field seems Eden, and each calm retreat;
Each village seems the haunt of holy feet.

But that sweet village, where my black-eyed
    maid
Closes her eyes in sleep beneath night's shade,
Whene'er I enter, more than mortal fire
Burns in my soul, and does my song inspire.

SONG.

WHEN early morn walks forth in sober
    grey,
Then to my black-eyed maid I haste away
When evening sits beneath her dusky bower,
And gently sighs away the silent hour,
The village bell alarms, away I go,
And the vale darkens at my pensive woe.

To that sweet village where my black-eyed
    maid
Doth drop a tear beneath the silent shade
I turn my eyes ; and pensive as I go,
Curse my black stars, and bless my pleasing
    woe.

Oft, when the summer sleeps among the trees,
Whispering faint murmurs to the scanty breeze,
I walk the village round ; if at her side
A youth doth walk in stolen joy and pride,
I curse my stars in bitter grief and woe,
That made my love so high, and me so low.

Oh, should she e'er prove false, his limbs I'd
   tear
And throw all pity on the burning air !
I'd curse bright fortune for my mixed lot,
And then I'd die in peace, and be forgot.

TO THE MUSES.

WHETHER on Ida's shady brow,
   Or in the chambers of the East,
The chambers of the Sun, that now
   From ancient melody have ceased ;

Whether in heaven ye wander fair,
   Or the green corners of the earth,
Or the blue regions of the **air**
   Where the melodious winds have birth ;

Whether on crystal rocks ye rove,
   Beneath the bosom of the sea,
Wandering in many a coral grove ;
   Fair Nine, forsaking Poetry ;

How have you left the ancient love
   That bards of old enjoyed in you !
The languid strings do scarcely move,
   The sound is forced, the notes are few !

AN IMITATION OF SPENSER.

GOLDEN Apollo, that through heaven wide
  Scatter'st the rays of light, and truth his
   beams,
In lucent words my darkling voices dight,
  And wash my earthly mind in thy clear
   streams,
  That wisdom may descend in fairy dreams,
All while the jocund hours in thy train
  Scatter their fancies at thy poet's feet ;
And, when thou yield'st to night thy wide
   domain,
  Let rays of truth enlight his sleeping brain.

For brutish Pan in vain might thee assay
  With tinkling sounds to dash thy nervous
   verse,
Sound without sense ; yet in his rude affray
  (For Ignorance is Folly's leasing nurse,
  And love of Folly needs none other's curse)
Midas the praise hath gained of lengthened
   ears,
  For which himself might deem him ne'er
   the worse
To sit in council with his modern peers,
  And judge of tinkling rhymes and elegances
   terse.

And thou, Mercurius, that with winged bow
  Dost mount aloft into the yielding sky,
And through Heaven's halls thy airy flight
    dost throw,
  Entering with holy feet to where on high
  Jove weighs the counsel of futurity ;
Then laden with eternal fate, dost go
  Down, like a fallen star, from Autumn sky,
  And o'er the surface **of the** silent deep dost
    fly :

If thou arrivest at the sandy shore
  Where nought **but** envious hissing adders
    dwell,
Thy golden rod thrown on the dusty floor,
  Can charm to harmony with potent **spell** ;
  Such **is sweet** Eloquence, **that does dispel**
Envy and Hate **that** thirst for human gore ;
  And cause in sweet society to dwell
  Vile savage minds that lurk in lonely cell.

O Mercury, assist my labouring sense
  That round the circle of the world would fly,
As the winged eagle **scorns** the towery fence
  Of Alpine hills round his high aëry,
  And searches through the corners of the sky,
Sports in the clouds to hear the thunder's sound,
  And see the winged lightnings as they fly ;
Then, bosomed in an amber cloud, around
  Plumes his wide wings, and seeks Sol's
    palace high.

                        B

And thou, O warrior Maid invincible,
 Armed with the terrors of Almighty Jove,
Pallas, Minerva, maiden terrible,
 Lov'st thou to **walk the** peaceful solemn
  grove,
In solemn gloom of branches interwove?
Or bear'st thy Ægis o'er the burning field
 Where like the sea the waves of battle
  move?
Or have thy soft piteous eyes beheld
 The weary wanderer through the desert
  rove?
Or does the afflicted man thy heavenly bosom
  move?

KING EDWARD THE THIRD.

PERSONS.

KING EDWARD.	SIR THOMAS DAGWORTH.
THE BLACK PRINCE.	SIR WALTER MANNY.
QUEEN PHILIPPA.	LORD AUDLEY.
DUKE OF CLARENCE.	LORD PERCY.
SIR JOHN CHANDOS.	BISHOP.

WILLIAM, *Dagworth's man.*

PETER BLUNT, *a common soldier.*

SCENE.—*The Coast of France.*

KING EDWARD *and Nobles before it.   The Army.*

KING.

O THOU, to whose fury the nations are
    But as dust ! maintain thy servant's
      right.
Without thine aid, the twisted mail, and spear,
And forged helm, and shield of seven-times
    beaten brass
Are idle trophies of the vanquisher.
When confusion rages, when the field is in a
    flame,
When **the cries of** blood tear horror from
    heaven,
And yelling death runs up and down the
    ranks,

Let Liberty, the chartered right of Englishmen,
Won by our fathers in many a glorious field,
Enerve my soldiers ; let Liberty
Blaze in each countenance, and fire the battle.
The enemy fight in chains, invisible chains,
    but heavy ;
Their minds are fettered ; then how can they
    be free ?
While, like the mounting flame,
We spring to battle o'er the floods of death !
And these fair youths, the flower of England,
Venturing their lives in my most righteous
    cause,
Oh, sheathe their hearts with triple steel, that
    they
May emulate their fathers' virtues !
And thou, my son, be strong ; thou fightest
    for a crown
That death can never ravish from thy brow,
A crown of glory—but from thy very dust
Shall beam a radiance, to fire the breasts
Of youth unborn !   Our names are written
    equal
In Fame's wide-trophied hall ; 'tis ours to
    gild
The letters, and to make them shine with
    gold
That never tarnishes : whether Third Edward,
Or the Prince of Wales, or Montacute, or
    Mortimer,

Or ev'n the least by birth, shall gain the
    brightest fame,
Is in His hand to whom all men are equal.
The world of men are like the numerous stars
That beam and twinkle in the depth of night,
Each clad in glory according to his sphere ;
But we, that wander from our native seats
And beam forth lustre on a darkling world,
Grow large as we advance : and some, perhaps,
The most obscure at home, that scarce were
    seen
To twinkle in their sphere, may so advance
That the astonished world, with upturned eyes,
Regardless of the moon, and those that once
    were bright,
Stand only for to gaze upon their splendour.

         [He here knights the Prince and
              other young nobles.

Now let us take a just revenge for those
Brave Lords who fell beneath the bloody axe
At Paris. Thanks, noble Harcourt, for 'twas
By your advice we landed here in Brittany,
A country not yet sown with destruction,
And where the fiery whirlwind of swift war
Has not yet swept its desolating wing.
Into three parties we divide by day,
And separate march, but join again at night :
Each knows his rank, and Heaven marshal all.

                    [Exeunt.

SCENE.—*English Court.*

LIONEL, DUKE OF CLARENCE, QUEEN PHILIPPA,
Lords, Bishops, &c.

CLARENCE.

My Lords, I have by the advice of her
Whom I am doubly bound to obey, my Parent
And my Sovereign, called you together.
My task is great, my burden heavier than
My unfledged years ;
Yet with your kind assistance, Lords, I hope
England shall dwell in peace : that, while my
    father
Toils in his wars, and turns his eyes on this
His native shore, and sees commerce fly round
With his white wings, and sees his golden
    London
And her silver Thames thronged with shining
    spires
And corded ships, her merchants buzzing
    round
Like summer bees, and all the golden cities
In his land overflowing with honey,
Glory may not be dimmed with clouds of care.
Say, Lords, should not our thoughts be first to
    commerce ?
My Lord Bishop, you would recommend us
    agriculture ?

BISHOP.

Sweet Prince, the arts of peace are great,
And no less glorious than those of war,
Perhaps more glorious in the philosophic mind.
When I sit at my home, a private man,
My thoughts are on my gardens and my fields,
How to employ the hand that lacketh bread.
If Industry is in my diocese,
Religion will flourish ; each man's heart
Is cultivated, and will bring forth fruit :
This is my private duty and my pleasure.
But, as I sit in council with my prince,
My thoughts take in the general good of the
    whole,
And England is the land favoured by Com-
    merce ;
For Commerce, though the child of Agri-
    culture,
Fosters his parent, who else must sweat and
    toil,
And gain but scanty fare. Then my dear
    Lord,
Be England's trade our care ; and we as
    tradesmen
Looking to the gain of this our native land.

CLARENCE.

O my good Lord, true wisdom drops like
    honey

From your tongue, as from a worshipped
    oak !
Forgive, my Lords, my talkative youth, that
    speaks
Not merely what my narrow observation has
Picked up, but what I have concluded from
    your lessons.
Now, by the Queen's advice, I ask your leave
To dine to-morrow with the Mayor of London :
If I obtain your leave, I have another boon
To ask, which is the favour of your company.
I fear Lord Percy will not give me leave.

PERCY.

Dear Sir, a prince should always keep his
    state,
And grant his favours with a sparing hand,
Or they are never rightly valued.
These are my thoughts : yet it were best to go:
But keep a proper dignity, for now
You represent the sacred person of
Your father ; 'tis with princes as 'tis with the
    sun ;
If not sometimes o'erclouded, we grow weary
Of his officious glory.

CLARENCE.

Then you will give me leave to shine some-
    times,
My Lord ?

LORD.

Thou hast a gallant spirit which I fear
Will be imposed on by the closer sort.

[*Aside.*

CLARENCE.

Well, I'll endeavour to take
Lord Percy's advice ; I have been used so
    much
To dignity that I'm sick on't.

QUEEN PHILIPPA.

Fie, fie, Lord Clarence ! you proceed not to
    business,
But speak of your own pleasures.
I hope their lordships will excuse your giddi-
    ness.

CLARENCE.

My Lords, the French have fitted out many
Small ships of war that, like to raving wolves
Infest our English seas, devouring all
Our burdened vessels, spoiling our naval flocks.
The merchants do complain, and beg our aid.

PERCY.

The merchants are rich enough ;
Can they not help themselves ?

BISHOP.

They can, and may ; but how to gain their will
Requires our countenance and help.

PERCY.

When that they find they must, my Lord, they
   will.
Let them but suffer awhile, and you shall see
They will bestir themselves.

BISHOP.

Lord Percy cannot mean that we should suffer
This disgrace.   If so, we are not sovereigns
Of the sea—our right, that heaven gave
To England, when at the birth of Nature
She was seated in the deep ; the Ocean ceased
His mighty roar, and, fawning, played around
Her snowy feet, and owned his awful Queen.
Lord Percy, if the heart is sick, the head
Must be aggrieved ; if but one member suffer,
The heart doth fail.   You say, my Lord, the
   merchants
Can, if they will, defend themselves against
These rovers : this is a noble scheme,
Worthy the brave Lord Percy, and as worthy
His generous aid to put it into practice.

PERCY.

Lord Bishop, what was rash in me is wise
In you ; I dare not own the plan.   'Tis not
Mine.   Yet will I, if you please,
Quickly to the Lord Mayor, and work him
   onward

To this most glorious voyage ; on which cast.
I'll set my whole estate,
But we will bring these Gallic rovers under.

QUEEN PHILIPPA.

Thanks, **brave** Lord Percy ; **you have the**
thanks
Of England's Queen, and will, ere long, of
England. [*Exeunt.*

SCENE.—*At Cressy.*

Sir Thomas Dagworth *and* Lord Audley
meeting.

AUDLEY.

Good-morrow, brave Sir Thomas ; the bright
morn
Smiles on our army, **and** the gallant sun
Springs from the hills like a young hero
Into the battle, shaking his golden locks
Exultingly : this is a promising day.

DAGWORTH.

Why, my Lord Audley, I don't know.
Give me your hand, and now I'll tell you what
I think you do not know. Edward's afraid of
Philip.

AUDLEY.

Ha, ha ! Sir Thomas ! you but joke ;
Did you e'er see **him** fear ? At Blanchetaque,

When almost singly he drove six thousand
French from the ford, did he fear then?

DAGWORTH.

Yes, fear—that made him fight so.

AUDLEY.

By the same reason I might say 'tis fear
That makes you fight.

DAGWORTH.

Mayhap you may. Look upon Edward's face,
No one can say he fears ; but, when he turns
His back, then I will say it to his face ;
He is afraid : he makes us all afraid.
I cannot bear the enemy at my back.
Now here we are at Cressy ; where to-morrow,
To-morrow we shall know. I say, Lord
    Audley,
That Edward runs away from Philip.

AUDLEY.

Perhaps you think the Prince, too, is afraid?

DAGWORTH.

No ; God forbid ! I'm sure he is not.
He is a young lion. Oh, I have seen him fight
And give command, and lightning has flashed
From his eyes across the field : I have seen him
Shake hands with death, and strike a bargain
    for

The enemy ; he has danced in the field
Of battle, like the youth at morris-play.
I'm sure he's not afraid, nor Warwick, nor none,
None of us but me, and I am very much afraid.

AUDLEY.

Are you afraid, too, Sir Thomas ?
I believe that as much as I believe
The King's afraid : but what are you afraid of ?

DAGWORTH.

Of having my back laid open ; we turn
Our backs to the fire, till we shall burn our
 skirts.

AUDLEY.

And this, Sir Thomas, you call fear ? Your
 fear
Is of a different kind, then, from **the** King's :
He fears to turn his face, and you to turn your
 back.
I do not think, Sir Thomas, you know what
 fear is.

Enter SIR JOHN CHANDOS.

CHANDOS.

Good-morrow, Generals ; I give you joy :
Welcome to the fields of Cressy. Here we
 stop,
And wait for Philip.

DAGWORTH.

I hope so.

AUDLEY.

There, Sir Thomas ; do you call that fear ?

DAGWORTH.

I don't know ; perhaps he takes it by fits.
Why, noble Chandos, look you here—
One rotten sheep spoils the whole flock ;
And if the bell-wether is tainted, I wish
The Prince may not catch the distemper too.

CHANDOS.

Distemper, Sir Thomas ! what distemper?
I have not heard.

DAGWORTH.

Why, Chandos, you are a wise man,
I know you understand me ; a distemper
The King caught here in France of running
        away.

AUDLEY.

Sir Thomas, you say you have caught it too.

DAGWORTH.

And so will the whole army ; 'tis very catching,
For, when the coward runs, the brave man
        totters.

Perhaps the air of the country is the cause.
I feel it coming upon me, so I strive against it ;
You yet are whole ; but, after a few more
Retreats, we all shall know how to retreat
Better than fight.—To be plain, I think re-
    treating
Too often takes away a soldier's courage.

CHANDOS.

Here comes the King himself : tell him your
    thoughts
Plainly, Sir Thomas.

DAGWORTH.

I've told him before, but his disorder
Makes him deaf.

Enter KING EDWARD *and* BLACK PRINCE.

KING.

Good-morrow, Generals ; when English cour-
    age fails,
Down goes our right to France.
But we are conquerors everywhere ; nothing
Can stand our soldiers ; each man is worthy
Of a triumph.   Such an army of heroes
Ne'er shouted to the heavens, nor shook the
    field.
Edward, my son, thou art
Most happy, having such command : the man

Were base who were not fired to deeds
Above heroic, having such examples.

PRINCE.

Sire, with respect and deference I look
Upon such noble souls, and wish myself
Worthy the high command that Heaven and
    you
Have given me. When I have seen the field
    glow,
And in each countenance the soul of war
Curbed by the manliest reason, I have been
    winged
With certain victory ; and 'tis my boast,
And shall be still my glory, I was inspired
By these brave troops.

DAGWORTH.

    Your Grace had better make them
All Generals.

KING.

Sir Thomas Dagworth, you must have your
    joke,
And shall, while you can fight as you did at
The Ford.

DAGWORTH.

I have a small petition to your Majesty.

KING.

What can Sir Thomas Dagworth ask
That Edward can refuse ?

DAGWORTH.

I hope your Majesty cannot refuse so great
A trifle ; I've gilt your cause with my best
    blood,
And would again, were I not forbid
By him whom I am bound to obey : my hands
Are tied up, my courage shrunk and withered,
My sinews slackened, and my voice scarce
    heard ;
Therefore I beg I may return to England.

KING.

I know not what you could have asked, Sir
    Thomas,
That I would not have sooner parted with
Than such **a** soldier **as** you have been, **and
    such a friend :**
Nay, I will know the most remote particulars
Of this your strange petition ; that, if I can,
I still may keep you here.

DAGWORTH.

Here on the fields of Cressy we are settled
Till Philip springs the timorous covey again.
The wolf is hunted down by causeless fear ;
The lion flees, and fear usurps his heart,
Startled, astonished at the clamorous cock ;
The eagle, that doth gaze upon the sun,
Fears the small fire that plays about the fen.
                  C

If at this moment of their idle fear
The dog doth seize the wolf, the forester the lion,
The negro in the crevice of the rock
Doth seize the soaring eagle ; undone by flight,
They tame submit : such the effect flight has
On noble souls.   Now hear its opposite :
The timorous stag starts from the thicket wild,
The fearful crane springs from the splashy fen,
The shining snake glides o'er the bending grass.
The stag turns head, and bays the crying
    hounds ;
The crane o'ertaken fighteth with the hawk ;
The snake doth turn, and bite the padding foot.
And if your Majesty's afraid of Philip,
You are more like a lion than a crane :
Therefore I beg I may return to England.

KING.

Sir Thomas, now I understand your mirth,
Which often plays with wisdom for its pastime,
And brings good counsel from the breast of
    laughter.
I hope you'll stay and see us fight this battle,
And reap rich harvest in the fields of Cressy ;
Then go to England, tell them how we fight,
And set all hearts on fire to be with us.
Philip is plumed, and thinks we flee from him,
Else he would never dare to attack us.   Now,
Now the quarry's set ! and death doth sport
In the bright sunshine of this fatal day.

DAGWORTH.

Now my heart dances, and I am as light
As the young bridegroom going to be married.
Now must I to my soldiers, get them ready,
Furbish our armours bright, new-plume our
    helms ;
And we will sing like the young housewives
    busied
In the dairy.   My feet are wing'd, but not
For flight, **an please** your grace.

KING.

If all my soldiers are as pleased as you,
'Twill be a gallant thing to fight or die ;
Then I can never be afraid of Philip.

DAGWORTH.

A raw-boned fellow t'other day passed by me ;
I told him to put off his hungry looks—
He answered me, " I hunger for another battle."
I saw a little Welshman with a fiery face ;
I told him **he** looked like **a** candle half
Burned out ; he answered, he was "*pig* enough
To light another *pattle*."   Last night, beneath
The moon I walked abroad, when all had
    pitched
Their tents, and all were still ;
I heard a blooming youth singing a song
He had composed, and at each pause he wiped

His dropping eyes. The ditty was, " if he
Returned victorious, he should wed a maiden
Fairer than snow, and rich as midsummer."
Another wept, and wished health to his father.
I chid them both, but gave them noble hopes.
These are the minds that glory in the battle,
And leap and dance to hear the trumpet sound.

KING.

Sir Thomas Dagworth, be thou near our
    person ;
Thy heart is richer than the vales of France :
I will not part with such a man as thee.
If Philip came armed in the ribs of death,
And shook his mortal dart against my head,
Thou'dst laugh his fury into nerveless shame !
Go now, for thou art suited to the work
Throughout the camp : inflame the timorous,
Blow up the sluggish into ardour, and
Confirm the strong with strength, the weak
    inspire,
And wing their brows with hope and expecta-
    tion :
Then to our tent return, and meet to council.
                    [*Exit* DAGWORTH.

CHANDOS.

That man's a hero in his closet, and more
A hero to the servants of his house
Than to the gaping world ; he carries windows

In that enlarged breast of his, that all
May see what's done within.

PRINCE.

He is a genuine Englishman, my Chandos,
And hath the spirit of Liberty within him.
Forgive my prejudice, Sir John ; I think
My Englishmen the bravest people on
The face of the earth.

CHANDOS.

Courage, my Lord, proceeds **from** self-depend-
ence.
Teach man to think he's a free agent,
Give but a slave his liberty, he'll shake
Off sloth, and build himself a hut, and hedge
A spot of ground ; this he'll defend ; 'tis his
By right of nature.   Thus set in action,
He will still move onward to plan conveniences,
Till glory fires his breast to enlarge his castle ;
While the poor slave drudges all day, in hope
To rest at night.

KING.

O Liberty, how glorious art thou !
I see thee hovering o'er my army, with
Thy wide-stretched plumes ; I see thee
Lead them on to battle ;
I see thee blow thy golden trumpet while
Thy sons shout the strong shout of victory !

O noble Chandos, think thyself a gardener,
My son a vine, which I commit unto
Thy care : prune all extravagant shoots, and
  guide
The ambitious tendrils in the path of wisdom ;
Water him with thy advice, and heaven
Rain freshening dew upon his branches ! And,
O Edward, my dear son ! learn to think lowly of
Thyself, as we may all each prefer other—
'Tis the best policy, and 'tis our duty.

[*Exit* KING EDWARD.

PRINCE.

And may our duty, Chandos, be our pleasure.—
Now we are alone, Sir John, I will unburden
And breathe my hopes into the burning air,
Where thousand deaths are posting up and
  down,
Commissioned to this fatal field of Cressy.
Methinks I see them arm my gallant soldiers,
And gird the sword upon each thigh, and fit
Each shining helm, and string each stubborn
  bow,
And dance to the neighing of our steeds.
Methinks the shout begins, the battle burns ;
Methinks I see them perch on English crests,
And roar the wild flame of fierce war upon
The thronged enemy ! In truth, I am too
  full ;
It is my sin to love the noise of war.

Chandos, thou seest my weakness; strong
    Nature
Will bend or break us: my blood, like a
    springtide,
Does rise so high to overflow all bounds
Of moderation; while Reason, in her frail
    bark,
Can see no shore or bound for vast ambition.
Come, take the helm, my Chandos,
That my full-blown sails overset me not
In the wild tempest. Condemn my venturous
    youth,
That plays with danger, as the innocent child,
Unthinking, plays upon the viper's den:
I am a coward in my reason, Chandos.

CHANDOS.

You are a man, my prince, and a brave man,
If I can judge of actions; but your heat
Is the effect of youth, and want of use:
Use makes the armed field and noisy war
Pass over as a summer cloud, unregarded,
Or but expected as a thing of course.
Age is contemplative; each rolling year
Brings forth fruit to the mind's treasure-house:
While vacant youth doth crave and seek about
Within itself, and findeth discontent,
Then, tired of thought, impatient takes the
    wing,
Seizes the fruits of time, attacks experience,

Roams round vast Nature's forest, where no
    bounds
Are set, the swiftest may have room, the
    strongest
Find prey ; till, tired at length, sated and tired
With the changing sameness, old variety,
We sit us down, and view our former joys
With distaste and dislike.

PRINCE.

Then, if we must tug for experience,
Let us not fear to beat round Nature's wilds,
And rouse the strongest prey : then, if we fall,
We fall with glory.   I know the wolf
Is dangerous to fight, not good for food,
Nor is the hide a comely vestment ; so
We have our battle for our pains.   I know
That youth has need of age to point fit prey,
And oft the stander-by shall steal the fruit
Of the other's labour.   This is philosophy ;
These are the tricks of the world ; but the pure
    soul
Shall mount on native wings, disdaining little
    sport,
And cut a path into the heaven of glory,
Leaving a track of light for men to wonder at.
I'm glad my father does not hear me talk ;
You can find friendly excuses for me, Chandos.
But do you not think, Sir John, that, if it
    please

The Almighty to stretch out my span of life,
I shall with pleasure view a glorious action
Which my youth mastered ?

CHANDOS.

Considerate age, my Lord, views motives,
And not acts ; when neither warbling voice
Nor trilling pipe is heard, nor pleasure sits
With trembling age, the voice of Conscience
    then,
Sweeter than music in a summer's eve,
Shall warble round the snowy head, and keep
Sweet symphony to feathered angels, sitting
As guardians round your chair ; then shall the
    pulse
Beat slow, and taste and touch and sight and
    sound and smell,
That sing and dance round Reason's fine-
    wrought throne,
Shall flee away, and leave him all forlorn ;
Yet not forlorn **if** Conscience is his friend.

> [*Exeunt.*

SCENE.—*In Sir Thomas Dagworth's Tent.*

DAGWORTH *and* WILLIAM, *his man.*

DAGWORTH.

Bring hither my armour, William.
Ambition is the growth of every clime.

WILLIAM.

Does it grow in England, sir?

DAGWORTH.

Ay, it grows most in lands most cultivated.

WILLIAM.

Then it grows most in France; the vines here
Are finer than any we have in England.

DAGWORTH.

Ay, but the oaks are not.

WILLIAM.

What is the tree you mentioned? I don't think
I ever saw it.

DAGWORTH.

Ambition.

WILLIAM.

Is it a little creeping root that grows in ditches?

DAGWORTH.

Thou dost not understand me, William.
It is a root that grows in every breast;
Ambition is the desire or passion that one man
Has to get before another, in any pursuit after
    glory;
But I don't think you have any of it.

WILLIAM.

Yes, I have; I have a great ambition to know everything, sir.

DAGWORTH.

But, when our first ideas are wrong, what follows must all be wrong, of course; 'tis best to know a little, and to know that little aright.

WILLIAM.

Then, sir, I should be glad to know if it was **not** ambition that brought over our King to France to fight for his right.

DAGWORTH.

Though the knowledge of that will not profit thee much, yet I will tell you that it was ambition.

WILLIAM.

Then, if ambition is a sin, we are all guilty in coming with him, and in fighting for him.

DAGWORTH.

Now, William, thou dost thrust the question **home** : but I must tell you that, guilt being an **act** of the mind, none are guilty but those whose minds are prompted by that same ambition.

WILLIAM.

Now, I always thought that a man might be
guilty of doing wrong without knowing it was
wrong.

DAGWORTH.

Thou art a natural philosopher, and knowst
truth by instinct ; while reason runs aground,
as we have run our argument. Only remember, William, all have it in their power to know
the motives of their own actions, and 'tis a sin
to act without some reason.

WILLIAM.

And whoever acts without reason may do a
great deal of harm without knowing it.

DAGWORTH.

Thou art an endless moralist.

WILLIAM.

Now there's a story come into my head, that
I will tell your honour, if you'll give me leave.

DAGWORTH.

No, William, save it till another time ; this
is no time for story-telling. But here comes
one who is as entertaining as a good story.

Enter PETER BLUNT.

PETER.

Yonder's a musician going to play before the King; it's a new song about the French and English, and the Prince has made the minstrel a squire, and given him I don't know what, and I can't tell whether he don't mention us all one by one; and he is to write another about all us that are to die, that we may be remembered in Old England, for all our blood and bones are in France; and a great deal more that we shall all hear by-and-by. And I came to tell your honour, because you love to hear war-songs.

DAGWORTH.

And who is this minstrel, Peter, dost know?

PETER.

Oh, ay, I forgot to tell that; he has got the same name as Sir John Chandos that the Prince is always with—the wise man that knows us all as well as your honour, only ain't so good-natured.

DAGWORTH.

I thank you, Peter, for your information, but not for your compliment, which is not true. There's as much difference between him and

me as between glittering sand and fruitful
mould ; or shining glass and a wrought diamond, set in rich gold, and fitted to the finger
of an Emperor ; such is that worthy Chandos.

PETER.

I know your honour does not think anything
of yourself, but everybody else does.

DAGWORTH.

Go, Peter, get you gone ; flattery is delicious,
even from the lips of a babbler.

[*Exit* PETER.

WILLIAM.

I never flatter your honour.

DAGWORTH.

I don't know that.

WILLIAM.

Why, you know, sir, when we were in
England, at the tournament at Windsor, and
the Earl of Warwick was tumbled over, you
asked me if he did not look well when he
fell ; and I said no, he looked very foolish ;
and you were very angry with me for not flattering you.

DAGWORTH.

You mean that I was angry with you for not
flattering the Earl of Warwick.

[*Exeunt.*

SCENE.—*Sir Thomas Dagworth's Tent.*

SIR THOMAS DAGWORTH. *To him enters* SIR
WALTER MANNY.

SIR WALTER.

Sir Thomas Dagworth, I have been weeping
Over the men that are to die to-day.

DAGWORTH.

Why, brave Sir Walter, you or I may fall.

SIR WALTER.

I know this breathing flesh must lie and rot,
Covered with silence and forgetfulness.
Death roams in cities' smoke, and in still night,
When men sleep in their beds, walketh about.
How many in walled cities lie and groan,
Turning themselves upon their beds,
Talking with death, answering his hard de-
    mands !
How many walk in darkness, terrors are round
The curtains of their beds, destruction is
Ready at the door ! How many sleep
In earth, covered with stones and deathy dust,
Resting in quietness, whose spirits **walk**
Upon the clouds of heaven, to **die no more !**
Yet death is terrible, though borne on angels'
    wings.

How terrible then is the field of death,
Where he doth rend the vault of heaven,
And shake the gates of hell !
O Dagworth, France is sick ! the very sky,
Though sunshine light it, seems to me as pale
As the pale fainting man on his death-bed,
Whose face is shown by light of sickly taper.
It makes me sad and sick at very heart ;
Thousands must fall to-day.

DAGWORTH.

Thousands of souls must leave this prison-
    house,
To be exalted to those heavenly fields
Where songs of triumph, palms of victory,
Where peace and joy and love and calm
    content,
Sit singing in the azure clouds, and strew
Flowers of heaven's growth over the banquet-
    table.
Bind ardent hope upon your feet like shoes,
Put on the robe of preparation !
The table is prepared in shining heaven,
The flowers of immortality are blown ;
Let those that fight fight in good steadfastness,
And those that fall shall rise in victory.

SIR WALTER.

I've often seen the burning field of war,
And often heard the dismal clang of arms ;

But never, till this fatal day of Cressy,
Has my soul fainted with these views **of** death ;
I seem to be in one great charnel-house,
And seem to scent the rotten carcases ;
I seem to hear the dismal yells of death,
While the black gore drops from his horrid
    jaws :
Yet I fear not the monster in his pride—
But oh ! the souls that are to die to-day !

DAGWORTH.

Stop, brave Sir Walter ; let me drop a tear,
Then let the clarion of war begin ;
I'll fight and weep, 'tis in my country's cause ;
I'll weep and shout for glorious liberty.
Grim war **shall** laugh and shout, decked **in**
    tears,
And blood shall flow like streams across the
    meadows,
That murmur down their pebbly channels,
    and
Spend their sweet lives to do their country
    service :
Then shall England's verdure shoot, her fields
    shall smile,
Her ships shall sing across the foaming sea,
Her mariners shall use the flute and viol,
And rattling guns, and black and dreary war,
Shall be **no** more.

SIR WALTER.

Well, let the trumpet sound, and the **drum**
    beat ;
Let war stain the blue heavens with **bloody**
    banners ;
I'll draw **my sword, nor ever** sheathe it up
Till England blow the trump of victory,
Or I lie stretched upon the field of death.

                  [*Exeunt.*

SONGS OF INNOCENCE.

1789.

INTRODUCTION.

PIPING down the valleys wild,
  Piping songs of pleasant glee,
On a cloud I saw a child,
  And he laughing said to me :

" Pipe a song about a Lamb !"
  So I piped with merry cheer.
" Piper, pipe that song again ; "
  So I piped : he wept to hear.

" Drop thy pipe, thy happy pipe ;
  Sing thy songs of happy cheer ! "
So I sang the same again,
  While he wept with joy to hear.

" Piper, sit thee down and write
  In a book that all may read."
So he vanished from my sight ;
  And I plucked a hollow reed,

And I made a rural pen,
  And I stained the water clear,
And I wrote my happy songs
  Every child may joy to hear.

THE SHEPHERD.

HOW sweet is the shepherd's **sweet lot** !
From the morn to the evening he **strays** ;
He shall follow his sheep all the day,
And his tongue shall be filled with praise.

For he hears the lambs' innocent call,
And he hears the ewes' tender reply ;
He is watchful while they are in peace,
For they know when their shepherd is nigh.

THE ECHOING GREEN.

THE sun does arise,
And make happy the skies ;
The merry bells ring,
To welcome the Spring ;
The skylark and thrush,
The birds of the bush,
Sing louder around
To the bells' cheerful sound ;
While our sports shall be **seen**
On the echoing green.

Old John, with white hair,
Does laugh away care,

Sitting under the oak,
Among the old folk.
They laugh at our play,
And soon they all say,
" Such, such were the joys
When we all—girls and boys—
In our youth-time were seen
On the echoing green."

Till the little ones, weary,
No more can be merry :
The sun does descend,
And our sports have an end.
Round the laps of their mothers
Many sisters and brothers,
Like birds in their nest,
Are ready for rest,
And sport no more seen
On the darkening green.

THE LAMB.

LITTLE lamb, who made thee ?
Dost thou know who made thee,
Gave thee life, and bade thee feed
By the stream and o'er the mead ;
Gave thee clothing of delight,
Softest clothing, woolly, bright ;

Gave thee such a tender voice,
Making all the vales rejoice?
  Little lamb, who made thee?
  Dost thou know who made thee?

  Little lamb, I'll tell thee;
  Little lamb, I'll tell thee:
He is called by thy name,
For He calls himself a lamb.
He is meek, and He is mild,
He became a little child.
I a child, and thou a lamb,
We are called by His name.
  Little lamb, God bless thee!
  Little lamb, God bless thee!

THE LITTLE BLACK BOY.

MY mother bore me in the southern wild,
  And I am black, but oh my soul is white,
White as an angel is the English child,
  But I am black, as if bereaved of light.

My mother taught me underneath a tree,
  And, sitting down before the heat of day,
She took me on her lap and kissed me,
  And, pointing to the East, began to say:

" Look on the rising sun : there God does live,
  And gives his light, and gives his heat away,
And flowers and trees and beasts and **men**
    receive
  Comfort in morning, joy in the noonday.

" And we are put on earth a little space,
  That we may learn to bear the beams **of**
    love ;
And these black bodies and this sunburnt face
  Are **but a** cloud, and like a shady grove.

" For, **when** our souls have learned the heat
    to bear,
  The cloud will vanish, we shall hear his
    voice,
Saying, ' Come **out** from the grove, **my love**
    and care,
  And round my golden tent like lambs
    rejoice.' "

Thus did my mother say, and kissed me,
  And thus I say to little English boy.
When **I** from black, and he from white cloud
    free,
  And round the tent of God like lambs we joy,

I'll shade him from the heat till he can bear
  To lean in joy upon our Father's knee ;
And then I'll stand and stroke his silver hair,
  And be like him, and he will then love me.

THE BLOSSOM.

MERRY, merry sparrow !
    Under leaves so green
A happy blossom
Sees you, swift as arrow,
Seek your cradle narrow,
Near my bosom.

Pretty, pretty robin !
Under leaves so green
A happy blossom
Hears you sobbing, sobbing,
Pretty, pretty robin,
Near my bosom.

THE CHIMNEY-SWEEPER.

WHEN my mother died I was very young,
    And my father sold me while yet my
        tongue
Could scarcely cry, "Weep! weep! weep!
    weep !"
So your chimneys I sweep, and in soot I sleep.

There's little Tom Dacre, who cried **when his**
    head,
That curled like a lamb's back, was shaved ;
    so I said,

" Hush, Tom ! never mind it, **for,** when your
    head's bare,
You know that the soot cannot spoil your **white**
    hair."

And so he was quiet, and that very night,
As Tom was a-sleeping, he had such a sight !—
That thousands of sweepers, Dick, Joe, Ned,
    and Jack,
Were all of them **locked** up in coffins of black.

And by came an angel, who had a bright key,
And he opened the coffins and set them all
    free ;
Then down a green plain, leaping, laughing,
    they run,
And wash **in a river, and shine in the sun.**

Then naked and white, all their bags left
    behind,
They rise upon clouds, and sport in the wind ;
And the angel told Tom, if he'd be a good boy,
He'd have God for his father, and never want
    joy.

And so **Tom** awoke, and we rose in the dark,
And got with our bags and our brushes to
    work.
Though the morning was cold, Tom was
    happy and warm :
So if all do their duty, they need not fear harm.

THE LITTLE BOY LOST.

FATHER, father, where are you going?
  Oh do not walk so fast!
Speak, father, speak to your little boy,
  Or else I shall be lost."

The night was dark, no father was there,
  The child was wet with dew;
The mire was deep, and the child did weep,
  And away the vapour flew.

THE LITTLE BOY FOUND.

THE little boy lost in the lonely fen,
  Led by the wandering light,
Began to cry, but God, ever nigh,
  Appeared like his father, in white.

He kissed the child, and by the hand led,
  And to his mother brought,
Who in sorrow pale, through the lonely dale,
  The little boy weeping sought.

LAUGHING SONG.

WHEN the green woods laugh with the
    voice of joy,
And the dimpling stream runs laughing by ;
When the air does laugh with our merry wit,
And the green hill laughs with the noise of it ;

When the meadows laugh with lively green,
And the grasshopper laughs in the merry
    scene ;
When Mary, and Susan, and Emily
With their sweet round mouths sing, " Ha,
    ha, he !"

When the painted birds laugh in the shade,
Where our table with cherries and nuts is
    spread :
Come live, and be merry, and join with me,
To sing the sweet chorus of " Ha, ha, he !"

A CRADLE SONG.

SWEET dreams, form a shade
    O'er my lovely infant's head !
Sweet dreams of pleasant streams
By happy, silent, moony beams !

Sweet sleep, with soft **down**
Weave thy brows an **infant crown** !
Sweet sleep, angel mild,
Hover o'er my happy child !

Sweet smiles, in the night
Hover over my delight !
Sweet smiles, mother's smile,
All the livelong night beguile.

Sweet moans, dovelike sighs,
Chase not slumber from thine eyes !
Sweet moan, sweeter smile,
All the dovelike moans beguile.

Sleep, sleep, happy child !
All creation slept and smiled.
Sleep, sleep, happy sleep,
While o'er thee doth mother weep.

Sweet babe, in thy face
Holy image I can trace ;
Sweet babe, once like thee
Thy Maker lay, and wept for me :

Wept for me, for thee, for all,
When He was an infant small.
Thou His image ever see,
Heavenly face that smiles on thee !

Smiles on thee, **on me,** on all,
Who became an **infant** small ;
Infant smiles are His own smiles :
Heaven **and** earth to peace beguiles.

THE DIVINE IMAGE.

TO Mercy, Pity, Peace, and Love,
    All pray in their distress,
And to these virtues of delight
    Return their thankfulness.

For Mercy, Pity, Peace, and Love,
    Is God our Father dear ;
And Mercy, Pity, Peace, and **Love,**
    Is man, his child and care.

For Mercy has a human heart ;
    Pity, **a** human face ;
And Love, the human form divine ;
    And Peace, the human dress.

Then every man, of every clime,
    That prays in his distress,
Prays to the human form divine :
    Love, Mercy, Pity, Peace.

And all must love the human form,
    In heathen, Turk, or Jew.
Where Mercy, Love, and Pity dwell,
    There God is dwelling too.

HOLY THURSDAY.

'TWAS on a Holy Thursday, their innocent
    faces clean,
Came children walking two and two, in red,
    and blue, and green :
Grey-headed beadles walked before, with
    wands as white as snow,
Till into the high dome of Paul's they like
    Thames waters flow.

Oh what a multitude they seemed, these
    flowers of London town !
Seated in companies they sit, with radiance
    all their own.
The hum of multitudes was there, but multi-
    tudes of lambs,
Thousands of little boys and girls raising their
    innocent hands.

Now like a mighty wind they raise to heaven
    the voice of song,
Or like harmonious thunderings the seats of
    heaven among :
Beneath them sit the aged men, wise guardians
    of the poor.
Then cherish pity, lest you drive an angel from
    your door.

NIGHT.

THE sun descending in the west,
　　The evening star does shine ;
The birds are silent in their nest,
And I must seek for mine.
　　The moon like a flower
　　In heaven's high bower,
　　With silent delight,
　　Sits and smiles on the night.

Farewell, green fields and happy grove,
Where flocks have ta'en delight.
Where lambs have nibbled, silent move
The feet of angels bright ;
　　Unseen, they pour blessing,
　　And joy without ceasing,
　　On each bud and blossom,
　　And each sleeping bosom.

They look in every thoughtless nest
Where birds are covered warm ;
They visit caves of every beast,
To keep them all from harm :
　　If they see any weeping
　　That should have been sleeping,
　　They pour sleep on their head,
　　And sit down by their bed.

E

When wolves and tigers howl for prey,
They pitying stand and weep,
Seeking to drive their thirst away,
And keep them from the sheep.
  But, if they rush dreadful,
  The angels, most heedful,
  Receive each mild spirit,
  New worlds to inherit.

And there the lion's ruddy eyes
Shall flow with tears of gold :
And pitying the tender cries,
And walking round the fold :
  Saying : " Wrath by His meekness,
  And, by His health, sickness,
  Are driven away
  From our immortal day.

" And now beside thee, bleating lamb,
I can lie down and sleep,
Or think on Him who bore thy name,
Graze after thee, and weep.
  For, washed in life's river,
  My bright mane for ever
  Shall shine like the gold,
  As I guard o'er the fold."

SPRING.

SOUND the flute !
    Now 'tis mute ;
Birds delight,
Day and night,
Nightingale,
In the dale,
Lark **in sky**—
Merrily,
Merrily, merrily to welcome in the year.

    Little boy,
Full of joy ;
Little girl,
Sweet and small,
Cock does crow,
So do you ;
Merry voice,
Infant noise ;
Merrily, merrily **to** welcome in the year.

    Little lamb,
Here I am ;
Come and lick
My white neck ;
Let me pull
Your soft wool ;
Let me kiss
Your soft face ;
Merrily, merrily we welcome in **the year.**

NURSE'S SONG.

WHEN the voices of children are heard
    on the green,
  And laughing is heard on the hill,
My heart is at rest within my breast,
  And everything else is still.
"Then come home, my children, the sun is
    gone down,
  And the dews of night arise ;
Come, come, leave off play, and let us away,
  Till the morning appears in the skies."

" No, no, let us play, for it is yet day,
  And we cannot go to sleep ;
Besides, in the sky the little birds fly,
  And the hills are all covered with sheep."
" Well, well, go and play till the light fades
    away,
  And then go home to bed."
The little ones leaped, and shouted, and
    laughed,
  And all the hills echoed.

INFANT JOY.

I HAVE no name ;
I am but two days old."
What shall I call thee ?
" I happy am,
Joy is my name,"
Sweet joy befall thee !

Pretty joy !
Sweet joy, but two days old.
Sweet joy I call thee ;
Thou dost smile,
I sing **the** while ;
Sweet joy befall thee !

A DREAM.

ONCE a dream did weave a shade
O'er my angel-guarded bed,
That an emmet lost its way
Where on grass methought I lay.

Troubled, wildered, and forlorn,
Dark, benighted, travel-worn,
Over many a tangled spray,
All heart-broke, I heard her say :

"Oh, my children ! do they cry,
Do they hear their father sigh?
Now they look abroad to see,
Now return and weep for me."

Pitying, I dropped a tear :
But I saw a glow-worm near,
Who replied, " What wailing wight
Calls the watchman of the night?

" I am set to light the ground,
While the beetle goes his round :
Follow now the beetle's hum ;
Little wanderer, hie thee home !"

ON ANOTHER'S SORROW.

CAN I see another's woe,
    And not be in sorrow too?
Can I see another's grief,
And not seek for kind relief?

Can I see a falling tear,
And not feel my sorrow's share?
Can a father see his child
Weep, nor be with sorrow filled?

Can a mother sit and hear
An infant groan, an infant fear?
No, no ! never can it be !
Never, never can it be !

And can He who smiles on all
Hear the wren with sorrows small,
Hear the small bird's grief and care
Hear the woes that infants bear—

And not sit beside the nest,
Pouring pity in their breast,
And not sit the cradle near,
Weeping tear on infant's tear?

And not sit both night and day,
Wiping all our tears away?
Oh no! never can it be!
Never, never can it be!

He doth give His joy to all:
He becomes an Infant small,
He becomes a Man of Woe,
He doth feel the sorrow too.

Think not thou canst sigh a sigh,
And thy Maker is not by:
Think not thou canst weep a tear,
And thy Maker is not near.

Oh, He gives to us His joy,
That our grief He may destroy!
Till our grief is fled and gone
He doth sit by us and moan.

THE VOICE OF THE ANCIENT BARD.

YOUTH of delight ! come hither
    And see the opening morn,
Image of Truth new-born.
Doubt is fled, and clouds of reason,
Dark disputes and artful teasing.
Folly is an endless maze ;
Tangled roots perplex her ways ;
How many have fallen there !
They stumble all night over bones of the dead ;
And feel—they know not what, but care ;
And wish to lead others, when they should be
    led.

SONGS OF EXPERIENCE.

1794.

INTRODUCTION.

HEAR the voice of the Bard,
    Who present, past, and future sees ;
Whose ears have heard
The Holy Word
That walked among the ancient trees ;

Calling the lapsed soul,
And weeping in the evening dew ;
That might control
The **starry pole,**
And fallen, **fallen** light renew !

"**O Earth,** O Earth, return !
Arise from out the dewy grass !
Night is worn,
And the morn
Rises from the slumb'rous mass.

"**Turn away** no more ;
Why wilt thou turn away?
The starry floor,
The watery shore,
Are given thee till the break of day."

EARTH'S ANSWER.

EARTH raised up her head
　　From the darkness dread and drear,
Her light fled,
Stony, dread,
And her locks covered with grey despair,

"Prisoned on watery shore,
Starry jealousy does keep my den
Cold and hoar :
Weeping o'er,
I hear the father of the ancient men,

" Selfish father of men !
Cruel, jealous, selfish fear !
Can delight,
Chained in night,
The virgins of youth and morning bear?

" Does spring hide its joy,
When buds and blossoms grow ?
Does the sower
Sow by night,
Or the ploughman in darkness plough ?

"Break this heavy chain,
That does freeze my bones around !
Selfish, vain,
Eternal bane,
That free love with bondage bound."

THE CLOD AND THE PEBBLE.

L OVE seeketh not itself to please,
　　Nor for itself hath any **care,**
But for another gives its ease,
　　And builds **a** heaven in hell's despair."

So sang a little clod of clay,
　Trodden with the cattle's feet.
But a pebble of the brook
　　Warbled out these metres meet :

" Love seeketh only *Self* to please,
　　To bind another to its delight,
Joys in another's loss of ease,
　　And builds a hell in heaven's despite."

HOLY THURSDAY.

I S this a holy thing to see
　　In a rich and fruitful land—
Babes reduced to misery,
　　Fed with cold and usurous hand ?

Is that trembling cry a song ?
　　Can it be a song of joy ?
And so many children poor ?
　　It is a land of poverty !

And their sun does never shine,
  And their fields are bleak and bare,
And their ways are filled with thorns :
  It is eternal winter there.

For where'er the sun does shine,
  And where'er the rain does fall,
Babes should never hunger there,
  Nor poverty the mind appal.

THE LITTLE GIRL LOST.

I N futurity
    I prophetic see
That the earth from sleep
(Grave the sentence deep)

Shall arise and seek
For her Maker meek ;
And the desert wild
Become a garden mild.

In the southern clime,
Where the Summer's prime
Never fades away,
Lovely Lyca lay.

Seven summers old
Lovely Lyca told.
She had wandered long,
Hearing wild birds' song.

" Sweet sleep, come to me
Underneath this tree ;
Do father, mother, weep?
Where can Lyca sleep?

" Lost in desert wild
Is your little child.
How can Lyca sleep
If her mother weep ?

" If her heart does ache,
Then let Lyca wake ;
If my mother sleep,
Lyca shall **not weep.**

" Frowning, frowning night,
O'er this desert bright
Let thy moon arise,
While I close my eyes."

Sleeping Lyca lay
While the beasts of prey,
Come from caverns deep,
Viewed the maid asleep.

The kingly lion stood,
And the virgin viewed :
Then he gambolled round
O'er the hallowed ground

Leopards, tigers play
Round her as she lay ;
While the lion old
Bowed his mane of gold,

And her breast did lick,
And upon her neck,
From his eyes of flame,
Ruby tears there came ;

While **the lioness**
Loosed her slender dress,
And naked they conveyed
To caves **the** sleeping maid.

THE LITTLE GIRL **FOUND**.

A LL the night in woe
　　Lyca's parents go
Over valleys deep,
While the deserts **weep**.

Tired and woe-begone,
Hoarse with making moan,
Arm in arm, seven days
They traced the desert ways.

Seven nights they sleep
Among shadows deep,
And dream they see their child
Starved in desert wild.

Pale through pathless ways
The fancied image strays,
Famished, weeping, weak,
With hollow piteous shriek.

Rising from unrest,
The trembling woman pressed
With feet of weary woe ;
She could no further go.

In his arms he bore
Her, armed with sorrow sore ;
Till before their way
A crouching lion lay.

Turning back was vain :
Soon his heavy mane
Bore them to the ground.
Then he stalked around,

Smelling to his prey ;
But their fears allay
When he licks their hands,
And silent by them stands.

They look upon his eyes,
Filled with deep surprise ;
And wondering behold
A spirit armed in gold.

F

On his head a crown,
On his shoulders down
Flowed his golden hair.
Gone was all their **care.**

" Follow me," he said ;
" Weep not for the maid ;
In my palace deep
Lyca lies asleep."

Then they followed
Where the vision **led,**
And saw their sleeping child
Among tigers wild.

**To this day they dwell
In a lonely dell,**
Nor fear the wolfish **howl**
Nor the lion's growl.

THE CHIMNEY SWEEPER.

A **LITTLE** black thing among the snow,
  Crying, "Weep ! weep !" in notes of
woe !
" Where are thy father and mother ?   Say !"—
" They **are** both gone up to the church to pray.

" Because I was happy upon the heath,
And smiled among the winter's snow,
They clothed me in the clothes of death,
And taught me to sing the notes of woe.

"And because I am happy and dance and sing,
They think they have done me no **injury**,
And are gone to praise God and his priest **and**
    king,
Who make up a heaven of our misery."

THE SICK ROSE.

O ROSE, **thou art sick !**
    The invisible worm,
That flies in the night,
    In the howling storm,
Has found out thy bed
    Of crimson joy,
And his dark secret **love**
    Does thy **life destroy.**

NURSE'S SONG.

WHEN the voices of children are heard on
    the green,
  And whisperings are in the dale,
The days **of** my youth **rise** fresh in my mind,
  My face turns green and pale.

Then come home, my children, the sun is gone
    down,
  And the dews of night arise ;
Your spring **and** your day are wasted in play,
  And your **winter and night** in disguise.

THE FLY.

LITTLE Fly,
    Thy summer's play
My thoughtless hand
Has brushed away.

Am not I
A fly like thee?
Or art not thou
A man like me?

For I dance,
And drink, and sing,
Till some blind hand
Shall brush my wing.

If thought is life
And strength and breath,
And the want
Of thought is death ;

Then am I
A happy fly,
If I live,
Or if I die.

THE ANGEL.

I DREAMT a dream! What can it
    mean?
And that I was a maiden Queen
Guarded by an Angel mild :
Witless woe was ne'er beguiled !

And I wept both night and day,
And he wiped my tears away ;
And I wept both day and night,
And hid from him my heart's delight.

So he took his wings, and fled ;
Then the morn blushed rosy red.
I dried my tears, and armed my fears
With ten thousand shields and spears.

Soon my Angel came again ;
I was armed, he came in vain ;
For the time of youth was fled,
And grey hairs were on my head.

THE TIGER.

TIGER, tiger, burning bright
　　In the forests of the night,
What immortal hand or eye
Could frame thy fearful symmetry?

In what distant deeps or skies
Burnt the fire of thine eyes?
On what wings dare he aspire?
What the hand dare seize the fire?

And what shoulder and what art
Could twist the sinews of thy heart?
And, when thy heart began to beat,
What dread hand and what dread feet?

What the hammer? what the chain?
In what furnace was thy brain?
What the anvil? what dread grasp
Dare its deadly terrors clasp?

When the stars threw down their spears,
And watered heaven with their tears,
Did He smile his work to see?
Did He who made the lamb make thee?

Tiger, tiger, burning bright
In the forests of the night,
What immortal hand or eye
Dare frame thy fearful symmetry?

TIGER, Tiger, burning bright,
   In the forests of the night,
What immortal hand or eye
Framed thy fearful symmetry?

In what distant deeps or skies
Burned that fire within thine eyes?
On what wings dared he aspire?
What the hand dared seize the fire?

And what shoulder and what art
Could twist the sinews of thy heart?
When thy heart began to beat,
What dread hand formed thy **dread feet?**

What the hammer, what the chain,
Knit thy strength and forged thy brain?
What the anvil? What dread grasp
Dared thy deadly terrors clasp?

When **the** stars threw down their spears,
And watered heaven with **their** tears,
Did He smile his work to see?
Did He who made the lamb make thee?

MY PRETTY ROSE TREE.

A FLOWER was offered to me,
　　Such a flower as May never bore ;
But I said, " I've a pretty rose tree,"
　　And I passed the sweet flower o'er.
Then I went to my pretty rose tree,
　　To tend her by day and by night ;
But my rose turned away with jealousy,
　　And her thorns were my only delight.

AH, SUNFLOWER.

A H, Sunflower, weary of time,
　　Who countest the steps of the sun ;
Seeking after that sweet golden clime
　　Where the traveller's journey is done ;

Where the Youth pined away with desire,
　　And the pale virgin shrouded in snow,
Arise from their graves, and aspire
　　Where my Sunflower wishes to go !

THE LILY.

T HE modest Rose puts forth a thorn,
　　The humble sheep a threat'ning horn ;
Where the Lily white shall in love delight,
Nor a thorn nor a threat stain her beauty
　　bright.

THE GARDEN OF LOVE.

I LAID me down upon a bank
  Where Love lay sleeping ;
I heard among the rushes dank
  Weeping, weeping.

Then I went to the heath and the wild,
  To the thistles and thorns of the waste ;
And they told me how they were beguiled,
  Driven out, and compelled to be chaste.

I went to the Garden of Love,
  And saw what I never had seen ;
A chapel was built in the midst,
  Where I used to play on the green.

And the gates of this chapel were shut,
  And " Thou shalt not " writ over the door ;
So I turned to the Garden of Love,
  That so many sweet flowers bore.

And I saw it was filled with graves,
  And tombstones where flowers should be ;
And priests in black gowns were walking their
    rounds,
And binding with briars my joys and desires.

THE LITTLE VAGABOND.

DEAR mother, dear mother, the Church is
        cold ;
But the Alehouse is healthy, and pleasant, and
    warm.
Besides, I can tell where I am used well ;
The poor parsons with wind like a blown
    bladder swell.

But, if at the Church they would give us some
        ale,
And a pleasant fire our souls to regale,
We'd sing and we'd pray all the livelong day,
Nor ever once wish from the Church to stray.

Then the Parson might preach, and drink, and
        sing,
And we'd be as happy as birds in the spring ;
And modest Dame Lurch, who is always at
    church,
Would not have bandy children, nor fasting,
    nor birch.

And God, like a father, rejoicing to see
His children as pleasant and happy as he,
Would have no more quarrel with the Devil or
    the barrel,
But kiss him, and give him both drink and
    apparel.

LONDON.

I WANDER through each chartered street,
   Near where the chartered Thames does
     flow,
A mark in every face I meet—
   Marks of weakness, marks of woe.

In every cry of every man,
   In every infant's cry of fear,
In every voice, in every ban,
   The mind-forged manacles I hear :

How the chimney-sweeper's cry
   Every blackening church appals,
And the hapless soldier's sigh
   Runs in blood down palace-walls.

But most, through midnight streets I hear
   How the youthful harlot's curse
Blasts the new-born infant's tear,
   And blights with plagues the marriage-
     hearse.

THE HUMAN ABSTRACT.

PITY would be no more
      If we did not make somebody poor
And Mercy no more could be
If all were as happy as we.

And mutual fear brings Peace,
Till the selfish loves increase ;
Then Cruelty knits a snare,
And spreads his baits with care.

He sits down with holy fears,
And waters the ground with tears ;
Then Humility takes its root
Underneath his foot.

Soon spreads the dismal shade
Of Mystery over his head,
And the caterpillar and fly
Feed on the Mystery.

And it bears the fruit of Deceit,
Ruddy and sweet to eat,
And the raven his nest has made
In its thickest shade.

The gods of the earth and sea
Sought through nature to find this tree,
But their search was all in vain :
There grows one in the human Brain.

INFANT SORROW.

M Y mother groaned, my father wept :
    Into the dangerous **world I leapt,**
Helpless, naked, piping loud,
Like **a** fiend hid in a cloud.

Struggling in my father's hands,
Striving against my swaddling-bands,
Bound and weary, I thought best
To sulk upon my mother's **breast.**

THE POISON TREE.

I WAS angry with my friend :
    I told my wrath, my wrath did end.
I was angry with my foe :
I told it not, my wrath did grow.

And I watered it in **fears**
Night and morning with my tears,
And I sunned it with smiles
And with soft deceitful wiles.

And it grew both day and night
Till it bore an apple bright,
And my foe beheld it shine,
And he knew that it was mine,—

And into my garden stole
When the night had veiled the pole ;
In the morning, glad, I see
My foe outstretched beneath the tree.

A LITTLE BOY LOST.

NOUGHT loves another as itself,
  Nor venerates another so,
Nor is it possible to thought
  A greater than itself to know.

" And, father, how can I love you
  Or any of my brothers more ?
I love you like the little bird
  That picks up crumbs around the door."

The Priest sat by and heard the child ;
  In trembling zeal he seized his hair,
He led him by his little coat,
  And all admired the priestly care.

And standing on the altar high,
  " Lo, what a fiend is here ! " said he :
" One who sets reason up for judge
  Of our most holy mystery."

The weeping child could not be heard,
  The weeping parents wept in vain :
They stripped him to his little shirt,
  And bound him in an iron chain,

And burned him in a holy place
  Where many had been burned before ;
The weeping parents wept in vain.
  Are such things done on Albion's shore ?

A LITTLE GIRL LOST.

CHILDREN of the future age,
  Reading this indignant page,
Know that in a former time
Love, sweet love, was thought a crime.

In the age of gold,
Free from winter's cold,
Youth and maiden bright,
To the holy light,
Naked in the sunny beams delight.

Once a youthful pair,
Filled with softest care,
Met in garden bright
Where the holy light
Had just removed the curtains of the
    night.

Then, in rising day,
On the grass they play ;
Parents were afar,
Strangers came not near,
And the maiden soon forgot her fear.

Tired with kisses sweet,
They agree to meet
When the silent sleep
Waves o'er heaven's deep,
And the weary tired wanderers weep.

To her father white
Came the maiden bright ;
But his loving look,
Like the holy book,
All her tender limbs with terror shook.

" Ona, pale and weak,
To thy father speak !
Oh, the trembling fear !
Oh, the dismal care
That shakes the blossoms of my hoary
    hair ! "

A DIVINE IMAGE.

CRUELTY has a human heart,
    And Jealousy a human face ;
Terror the human form divine,
    And Secrecy the human dress.

The human dress is forged iron,
    The human form a fiery forge,
The human face a furnace sealed,
    The human heart its hungry gorge.

THE SCHOOLBOY.

I LOVE to rise on a summer morn,
  When birds are singing on every tree ;
The distant **huntsman winds his horn,**
  And the skylark **sings** with **me :**
  Oh what sweet company !

But to go to school in **a** summer morn—
  Oh, it drives all joy away !
Under a cruel eye outworn,
  The little ones spend the day
  In sighing and dismay.

Ah, then at times **I** drooping sit,
  And spend many an anxious hour ;
Nor in my book can I take delight,
  Nor sit in learning's bower,
  Worn through with the dreary shower.

How can the bird that is born for joy
  Sit **in** a cage and sing ?
How can a child, when fears annoy,
  But droop his tender wing,
  And forget his youthful spring ?

Ah, father and mother, if buds are nipped,
  And blossoms blown away ;
And if the tender plants are stripped
  Of their joy in the springing day,
  By sorrow and care's dismay—

G

How shall the summer arise in joy,
   Or the summer fruits appear?
Or how shall we gather what griefs destroy,
   Or bless the mellowing year,
   When the blasts of winter appear?

TO TIRZAH.

WHATE'ER is born of mortal birth
   Must be consumed with the earth,
To rise from generation free :
Then what have I to do with thee?

The sexes sprang from shame and pride,
Blown in the morn, in evening died ;
But mercy changed death into sleep ;
The sexes rose to work and weep.

Thou, mother of my mortal part,
With cruelty didst mould my heart,
And with false self-deceiving tears
Didst bind my nostrils, eyes, and ears,

Didst close my tongue in senseless clay,
And me to mortal life betray.
The death of Jesus set me free :
Then what have I to do with thee?

THE BOOK OF THEL.

(1789.)

THEL'S MOTTO.

Does the Eagle know what is in the pit,
    Or wilt thou go ask the Mole?
Can wisdom be put in a silver rod,
    Or love in a golden bowl?

I.

THE Daughters of the Seraphim led round
    their sunny flocks—
All but the youngest: she in paleness sought
    the secret air,
To fade away like morning beauty from **her**
    mortal day.
Down by the river of Adona her soft voice is
    heard,
And thus her gentle lamentation falls **like**
    morning dew.
" O life of this our Spring ! why fades the lotus
    of the water?
Why fade these children of the Spring, born
    but to smile and fall?
Ah ! Thel is like a watery bow, and like a
    parting cloud,
Like a reflection in a glass, like shadows in
    the water,

Like dreams of infants, like a smile upon an
　　infant's face,
Like the dove's voice, like transient day, like
　　music in the air.
Ah! gentle may I lay me down, and gentle
　　rest my head,
And gentle sleep the sleep of death, and gentle
　　hear the voice
Of Him that walketh in the garden in the
　　evening time!"

The Lily of the Valley, breathing in the
　　humble grass,
Answered the lovely maid, and said : " I am a
　　watery weed,
And I am very small, and love to dwell in
　　lowly vales ;
So weak, the gilded butterfly scarce perches
　　on my head.
Yet I am visited from heaven ; and He that
　　smiles on all
Walks in the valley, and each morn over me
　　spreads His hand,
Saying, ' Rejoice, thou humble grass, thou
　　new-born lily-flower,
Thou gentle maid of silent valleys and of
　　modest brooks ;
For thou shalt be clothed in light and fed
　　with morning manna,

Till summer's heat melts thee beside the
    fountains and the springs,
To flourish in eternal vales.' Then why should
    Thel complain?
Why should the mistress of the vales of **Har**
    utter a sigh?"

She ceased, and **smiled in** tears, then sat down
    in her silver shrine.

Thel answered : "O thou little virgin **of** the
    peaceful valley,
Giving **to** those that cannot crave, the voice-
    less, the o'ertired,
Thy breath doth nourish the innocent **lamb ;**
    he smells thy milky garments,
He crops thy flowers, while thou sittest smiling
    in his face,
Wiping his mild and meekin mouth from all
    contagious taints.
Thy wine **doth** purify the golden honey ; thy
    perfume,
Which **thou** dost scatter on every little blade
    of grass that springs,
Revives the milked cow, and tames the fire-
    breathing steed.
But Thel is like a faint cloud kindled at the
    rising sun :
I vanish from my pearly throne, and who shall
    find my place?"

" Queen of the vales," the Lily answered, "ask
    the tender Cloud,
And it shall tell thee why it glitters in the
    morning sky,
And why it scatters its bright beauty through
    the humid air.
Descend, O little Cloud, and hover before the
    eyes of Thel."

The Cloud descended ; and the Lily bowed
    her modest head,
And went to mind her numerous charge among
    the verdant grass.

II.

"O little Cloud," the virgin said, "I charge
    thee tell to me
Why thou complainest not, when in one hour
    thou fad'st away :
Then we shall seek thee, but not find. Ah !
    Thel is like to thee—
I pass away ; yet I complain, and no one hears
    my voice."

The Cloud then showed his golden head, and
    his bright form emerged,
Hovering and glittering on the air, before the
    face of Thel.

"O virgin, know'st thou not our steeds drink
of the golden springs
Where Luvah doth renew his horses ! Look'st
thou on my youth,
And fearest thou because I vanish and am
seen no more?
Nothing remains. O maid, I tell thee, when
I pass away,
It is to tenfold life, to love, to peace, and
raptures holy.
Unseen descending weigh my light wings
upon balmy flowers,
And court the fair-eyed Dew to take me to her
shining tent :
The weeping virgin trembling kneels before
the risen sun,
Till we arise, linked in a golden band, and
never part,
But walk united, bearing food to all our tender
flowers."

" Dost thou, O little Cloud? I fear that I am
not like thee ;
For I walk through the vales of Har, and
smell the sweetest flowers,
But I feed not the little flowers : I hear the
warbling birds,
But I feed not the warbling birds, they fly
and seek their food.

But Thel delights in these no more! because
    I fade away,
And all shall say, 'Without a use this shining
    woman lived,
Or did she only live to be at death the food of
    worms?'"

The Cloud reclined upon his airy throne, and
    answered thus :

" Then if thou art the food of worms, O virgin
    of the skies,
How great thy use, how great thy blessing !
    Everything that lives
Lives not alone nor for itself. Fear not, and
    I will call
The weak Worm from its lowly bed, and thou
    shalt hear its voice.
Come forth, Worm of the silent valley, to thy
    pensive queen."

The helpless Worm arose, and sat upon the
    Lily's leaf,
And the bright Cloud sailed on to find his
    partner in the vale.

III.

Then Thel, astonished, viewed the Worm upon
  its dewy bed.

" Art thou **a worm,** image of weakness? art
  thou but a worm ?
I **see** thee, like **an** infant, wrapped in the Lily's
  leaf.
Ah ! weep not, little voice ; thou canst not
  speak, but thou canst weep.
Is this **a** worm ? I see thee lie helpless and
  naked, weeping,
And none to answer, **none to** cherish thee with
  mother's smiles."

The Clod of Clay heard the Worm's voice,
  and raised her pitying head :
She bowed over the weeping infant, and her
  life exhaled
In milky fondness : then on Thel she fixed
  her humble eyes.

" O beauty of the vales of Har ! we live not
  for ourselves.
Thou seest me, the meanest thing, and so I
  am indeed.

My bosom of itself is cold, and of itself is
    dark ;
But He that loves the lowly pours His oil upon
    my head,
And kisses me, and binds His nuptial bands
    around my breast,
And says : 'Thou mother of my children, I
    have loved thee,
And I have given thee a crown that none can
    take away.'
But how this is, sweet maid, I know not, and
    I cannot know ;
I ponder, and I cannot ponder : yet I live and
    love ! "

The Daughter of Beauty wiped her pitying
    tears with her white veil,
And said : "Alas ! I knew not this, and there-
    fore did I weep.
That God would love a worm I knew, and
    punish the evil foot
That wilful bruised its helpless form ; but that
    He cherished it
With milk and oil I never knew, and therefore
    did I weep.
And I complained in the mild air, because I
    fade away,
And lay me down in thy cold bed, and leave
    my shining lot."

"Queen of the vales," the matron Clay
    answered, " I heard thy sighs,
And all thy moans flew o'er my roof, but I
    have called them down.
Wilt thou, O queen, enter my house ? 'Tis
    given thee to enter.
And to return : fear nothing, enter with thy
    virgin feet."

IV.

The eternal gates' terrific Porter lifted the
    northern bar ;
Thel entered in, and saw the secrets of the
    land unknown.
She saw the couches of the dead, and where
    the fibrous root
Of every heart on earth infixes deep its rest-
    less twists :
A land of sorrows and of tears, where never
    smile was seen.

She wandered in the land of clouds, through
    valleys dark, listening
Dolours and lamentations, wailing oft beside
    a dewy grave.
She stood in silence, listening to the voices of
    the ground,
Till to her own grave-plot she came, and there
    she sat down,
And heard this voice of sorrow breathed from
    the hollow pit.

" Why cannot the ear be closed to its own
  destruction ?
Or the glistening eye to the poison of a smile?
Why are eyelids stored with arrows ready
  drawn,
Where a thousand fighting-men in ambush lie,
Or an eye of gifts and graces showering fruits
  and coined gold?
Why a tongue impressed with honey from
  every wind?
Why an ear, a whirlpool fierce to draw crea-
  tions in?
Why a nostril wide inhaling terror, trembling,
  and affright?
Why a tender curb upon the youthful burning
  boy?
Why a little curtain of flesh on the bed of our
  desire ?"

The Virgin started from her seat, and with a
  shriek
Fled back unhindered till she came into the
  vales of Har.

THE GATES OF PARADISE.

(1793.)

MUTUAL forgiveness of each vice,
  Such are the Gates of Paradise,
Against the Accuser's chief desire,
Who walked among the stones of fire.
Jehovah's fingers wrote the Law :
He wept ; then rose in zeal and awe,
And, in the midst of Sinai's heat,
Hid it beneath His Mercy-Seat.
  O Christians ! Christians ! tell me why
You rear it on your altars high !

THE KEYS OF THE GATES.

THE caterpillar on the leaf
Reminds thee of thy mother's grief.
My Eternal Man set in repose,
The Female from his darkness rose ;
And she found me beneath a tree,
A mandrake, and in her veil hid me.
Serpent reasonings us entice
Of good and evil, virtue, vice.
Doubt self-jealous, watery folly,
Struggling through Earth's melancholy,

Naked in air, in shame, and fear,
Blind in fire, with shield and spear,
Two horrid reasoning cloven fictions,
In doubt which is self-contradiction,
A dark hermaphrodite I stood—
Rational truth, root of evil and good,
Round me, flew the flaming sword ;
Round her, snowy whirlwinds roared,
Freezing her veil, the mundane shell.
I rent the veil where the dead dwell :
When weary man enters his cave,
He meets his Saviour in the grave.
Some find a female garment there,
And some a male, woven with care,
Lest the sexual garments sweet
Should grow a devouring winding-sheet.
One dies ! alas ! the living and dead !
One is slain, and one is fled !
In vain-glory hatched and nursed,
By double spectres, self-accursed.
My son ! my son ! thou treatest me
But as I have instructed thee.
On the shadows of the moon,
Climbing through night's highest noon :
In Time's ocean falling, drowned :
In aged ignorance profound,
Holy and cold, I clipped the wings
Of all sublunary things :
And in depths of icy dungeons
Closed the father and the sons.

But, when once **I did** descry
The Immortal Man **that cannot die,**
Through evening shades I haste away
To close the labours of my day.
The door of Death **I** open found,
And the worm weaving in the ground :
Thou'rt my mother, from **the** womb ;
Wife, sister, daughter, to the tomb :
Weaving to dreams the sexual strife,
And weeping over the web of life.

DEDICATION OF THE DESIGNS TO BLAIR'S "GRAVE."

(1808.)

To Queen Charlotte.

THE door of Death is made of gold,
    That mortal eyes cannot behold :
But, when the mortal eyes are closed,
And cold and pale the limbs reposed,
The soul awakes, and, wondering, sees
In her mild hand the golden keys.
The grave is heaven's golden gate,
And rich and poor around it wait :
O Shepherdess of England's fold,
Behold this gate of pearl and gold !

To dedicate to England's Queen
The visions that my soul has seen,
And by her kind permission bring
What I have borne on solemn wing
From the vast regions of the grave,
Before her throne my wings I wave,
Bowing before my sovereign's feet.
The Grave produced these blossoms sweet,
In mild repose from earthly strife,
The blossoms of eternal life.

LATER POEMS.

H

AUGURIES OF **INNOCENCE**.

To see a world in a grain of sand,
And a heaven in a wild flower;
Hold infinity in the palm of your hand,
And eternity in an hour.

A **Robin** Redbreast in a cage
Puts all heaven in a rage ;
A dove-house filled with doves **and** pigeons
Shudders hell through all its regions.
A dog starved **at his** master's gate
Predicts the ruin of the state ;
A game-cock clipped and armed for fight
Doth the rising sun affright ;
A horse misused upon the road
Calls to heaven for human blood.
Every wolf's and lion's howl
Raises from hell a human soul ;
Each outcry of the hunted hare
A fibre from the brain doth tear ;
A skylark wounded on the wing
Doth make a cherub cease **to** sing.
He who shall hurt the little wren
Shall never be beloved by men ;

He who the ox to wrath has moved
Shall never be by woman loved ;
He who shall train the horse to war
Shall never pass the Polar Bar.
The wanton boy that kills the fly
Shall feel the spider's enmity ;
He who torments the chafer's sprite
Weaves a bower in endless night.
The caterpillar on the leaf
Repeats to thee thy mother's grief ;
The wild deer wandering here and there
Keep the human soul from care :
The lamb misused breeds public strife,
And yet forgives the butcher's knife.
Kill not the moth nor butterfly,
For the last judgment draweth nigh ;
The beggar's dog and widow's cat,
Feed them and thou shalt grow fat.
Every tear from every eye
Becomes a babe in eternity ;
The bleat, the bark, bellow and roar,
Are waves that beat on Heaven's shore.
The bat that flits at close of eve
Has left the brain that won't believe ;
The owl that calls upon the night
Speaks the unbeliever's fright.
The gnat that sings his summer's song
Poison gets from Slander's tongue ;
The poison of the snake and newt
Is the sweat of Envy's foot ;

The poison of the honey-bee
Is the artist's jealousy ;
The strongest poison ever known
Came from Cæsar's laurel-crown.

Nought can deform the human race
Like to the armourer's iron brace ;
The soldier armed with sword and gun
Palsied strikes the summer's sun.
When gold and gems adorn the plough,
To peaceful arts shall Envy bow.
The beggar's rags fluttering in air
Do to rags the heavens tear ;
The prince's robes and beggar's rags
Are toadstools on the miser's bags.
One mite wrung from the labourer's hands
Shall buy and sell the miser's lands,
Or, if protected from on high,
Shall that whole nation sell and buy ;
The poor man's farthing is worth more
Than all the gold on Afric's shore.
The whore and gambler, by the state
Licensed, build that nation's fate ;
The harlot's cry from street to street
Shall weave Old England's winding-sheet ;
The winner's shout, the loser's curse,
Shall dance before dead England's hearse.

He who mocks the infant's faith
Shall be mocked in age and death ;

He who shall teach the child to doubt
The rotten grave shall ne'er get out ;
He who respects the infant's **faith**
Triumphs over hell and death.
The babe is **more** than swaddling-bands
Throughout all these human lands ;
Tools were made, and born were hands,
Every farmer understands.
The questioner **who sits so sly**
Shall never know how to reply.
He who replies to words **of doubt**
Doth put the light of knowledge out ;
A puddle, or the cricket's cry,
Is to doubt a fit reply.
The child's toys and the old man's reasons
Are the fruits of the two seasons.
The emmet's inch and eagle's mile
Makes lame philosophy to smile.
A truth that's told with bad intent
Beats all the lies **you** can invent.
He who doubts from what he sees
Will ne'er believe, **do** what you please ;
If the sun and moon should doubt,
They'd immediately go out.

Every night and every morn
Some to misery are born ;
Every morn and every night
Some **are** born to sweet delight ;
Some are born to sweet delight,

Some are born to endless night.
Joy and woe are woven fine,
A clothing for the soul divine ;
Under every grief and pine
Runs a joy with silken twine.
It is right it should be so';
Man was made for joy and woe ;
And, when this we rightly know,
Safely through the world we go.

We are led to believe a lie
When we see *with* not *through* the eye,
Which was born in a night to perish in a night
When the soul slept in beams of light.
God appears and God is light
To those poor souls who dwell in night :
But doth a human form display
To those who dwell in realms of day.

THE MENTAL TRAVELLER.

I TRAVELLED through a land of men,
  A land of men and women too ;
And heard and saw such dreadful things
  As cold earth-wanderers never knew.

For there the babe is born in joy
  That was begotten in dire woe ;
Just as we reap in joy the fruit
  Which we in bitter tears did sow.

And, if the babe is born a boy,
  He's given to a woman old,
Who nails him down upon a rock,
  Catches his shrieks in cups of gold.

She binds iron thorns around his head,
  She pierces both his hands and feet,
She cuts his heart out at his side,
  To make it feel both cold and heat.

Her fingers number every nerve
  Just as a miser counts his gold ;
She lives upon his shrieks and cries,
  And she grows young as he grows old.

Till he becomes a bleeding youth,
  And she becomes a virgin bright ;
Then he rends up his manacles,
  And binds her down for his delight.

He plants himself in all her nerves
  Just as a husbandman his mould,
And she becomes his dwelling-place
  And garden fruitful seventyfold.

An aged shadow soon he fades,
  Wandering round an earthly cot,
Full-filled all with gems and gold
  Which he by industry had got.

And these are the gems of the human soul,
  The rubies and pearls of a lovesick eye,
The countless gold of the aching heart,
  The martyr's groan and the lover's sigh.

They are his meat, they are his drink ;
  He feeds the beggar and the poor ;
To the wayfaring traveller
  For ever open is his door.

His grief is their eternal joy,
  They make the roofs and walls to ring ;
Till from the fire upon the hearth
  A little female babe doth spring.

And she is all of solid fire
  And gems and gold, that none his hand
Dares stretch to touch her baby form,
  Or wrap her in his swaddling-band.

But she comes to the man she loves,
  If young or old or rich or poor ;
They soon drive out the aged host,
  A beggar at another's door.

He wanders weeping far away,
  Until some other take him in ;
Oft blind and age-bent, sore distressed,
  Until he can a maiden win.

And, to allay his freezing age,
    The poor man takes her in his arms ;
The cottage fades before his sight,
    The garden and its lovely charms.

The guests are scattered through the land ;
    For the eye altering alters all ;
The senses roll themselves in fear,
    And the flat earth becomes a ball.

The stars, sun, moon, all shrink away,
    A desert vast without a bound,
And nothing left to eat or drink,
    And a dark desert all around.

The honey of her infant lips,
    The bread and wine of her sweet smile,
The wild game of her roving eye,
    Do him to infancy beguile.

For as he eats and drinks he grows
    Younger and younger every day,
And on the desert wild they both
    Wander in terror and dismay.

Like the wild stag she flees away ;
    Her fear plants many a thicket wild,
While he pursues her night and day,
    By various arts of love beguiled ;

By various arts of love and hate,
  Till the wild desert's planted o'er
With labyrinths of wayward love,
  ` Where roam the lion, wolf, and boar.

Till he becomes a wayward babe,
  And she a weeping woman old ;
Then many **a** lover wanders here,
  The sun and stars are nearer rolled ;

The trees bring forth sweet ecstasy
  To all who in the desert roam ;
Till many a city there is built,
  And many a pleasant shepherd's home.

But, when they find the frowning **babe,**
  Terror strikes **through the** region wide :
They cry—" The babe—the babe is born !"
  And flee away on every side.

For who dare touch the frowning form,
  His arm is withered to its root :
Bears, lions, wolves, all howling flee,   .
  And every tree doth shed its fruit.

And none can touch that frowning form
  Except it be a woman old ;
She nails him down upon the rock,
  And all is done as I have told.

THE CRYSTAL CABINET.

THE maiden caught me in the wild,
   Where I was dancing merrily ;
She put me into her cabinet,
   And locked me up with a golden key.

This cabinet is formed of gold,
   And pearl and crystal shining bright,
And within it opens into a world
   And a little lovely moony night.

Another England there I saw,
   Another London with its Tower,
Another Thames and other hills,
   And another pleasant Surrey bower.

Another maiden like herself,
   Translucent, lovely, shining clear,
Threefold, each in the other closed—
   Oh what a pleasant trembling fear !

Oh, what a smile !   A threefold smile
   Filled me that like a flame I burned ;
I bent to kiss the lovely maid,
   And found a threefold kiss returned.

I strove to seize the inmost form
   With ardour fierce and hands of flame,
But burst the crystal cabinet,
   And like a weeping babe became :

A weeping babe upon the wild,
   And weeping woman pale reclined,
And in the outward air again
   I filled with woes the passing wind.

THE GOLDEN NET.

BENEATH a white-thorn's lovely May,
   Three virgins at the break of day,—
" Whither, young man, whither away?
Alas for woe ! alas for woe !"
They cry, and tears for ever **flow.**
The first was clothed in flames of fire,
The second clothed in iron wire ;
The third was clothed in tears and sighs,
Dazzling bright before my eyes.
They bore a net of golden twine
To hang upon the branches fine.
Pitying, I wept to see the woe
That love and beauty undergo—
To be clothed in burning fires
And in unsatisfied desires,
And in **tears** clothed night and day ;
It melted all my soul away.
When they saw my tears, a smile
That might heaven itself beguile
Bore the golden net aloft,
As on downy pinions soft,

Over the morning of my day.
Underneath the net I stray,
Now entreating Flaming-fire,
Now entreating Iron-wire,
Now entreating tears and sighs.—
Oh, when will the morning rise?

THE DEFILED SANCTUARY.

I SAW a chapel all of gold
    That none did dare to enter in,
And many weeping stood without,
    Weeping, mourning, worshipping.

I saw a serpent rise between
    The white pillars of the door,
And he forced and forced and forced
    Till he the golden hinges tore :

And along the pavement sweet,
    Set with pearls and rubies bright,
All his shining length he drew,
    Till upon the altar white

He vomited his poison out
    On the bread and on the wine.
So I turned into a sty,
    And laid me down among the swine.

SMILE AND FROWN.

THERE is a smile of Love,
    And there is a smile of Deceit,
And there is a smile of smiles
   In which the two smiles meet.

And there is a frown of Hate,
    And there is a frown of Disdain,
And there is a frown of frowns
   Which you strive to forget in vain,

For it sticks in the heart's deep core
   And it sticks in the deep backbone.
And no smile ever was smiled
   But only one smile alone

(And 'twixt the cradle and grave
   It only once smiled can be),
That when it once is smiled
   There's an end to all misery.

BROKEN LOVE.

M^Y Spectre around me night and **day**
　　Like a wild beast guards my way ;
My Emanation far within
Weeps incessantly for my sin.

A fathomless and boundless deep,
There we wander, there we weep ;
On the hungry craving wind
My Spectre follows thee behind.

He scents thy footsteps in the snow,
Wheresoever thou dost go ;
Through the wintry hail and rain
When wilt thou return again ?

Poor, pale, pitiable form,
That I follow in a storm,
From sin I never shall be free
Till thou forgive and come to me.

A deep winter, dark and cold,
Within my heart thou dost unfold ;
Iron tears and groans of lead
Thou bind'st around my aching head.

Dost thou not in pride and scorn
Fill with tempests all my morn,

And with jealousies and fears ?
And fill my pleasant nights with tears ?

O'er *my* sins thou dost sit and moan :
Hast thou **no** sins of thine own ?
O'er *my* sins thou dost sit and weep,
And lull thine own sins fast asleep.

Thy weeping thou shalt ne'er give o'er ;
I sin against **thee more and** more,
And never **will from** sin **be** free
Till thou forgive and come to me.

What transgressions I commit
Are for thy transgressions fit—
They, thy harlots, thou their slave ;
And my bed becomes their grave.

Seven of my sweet loves thy knife
Hath bereaved of their life :
Their marble tombs I built with tears
And with cold and shadowy fears.

Seven more loves weep night and day
Round the tombs where my loves lay,
And seven more loves attend at night
Around my couch with torches bright.

And seven more loves in my bed
Crown with vine my mournful head ;
Pitying and forgiving all
Thy transgressions, great and small.

I

When wilt thou return, and view
My loves, and them in life renew?
When wilt thou return and live?
When wilt thou pity as I forgive?

Throughout all eternity
I forgive you, you forgive me.
As our dear Redeemer said:
" This the wine, and this the bread."

THE EVERLASTING GOSPEL.

(Extract from the unfinished poem.)

WAS Jesus chaste? or did he
      Give any lessons of chastity?
The morning blushed **fiery** red;
Mary was found in adulterous bed.
Earth groaned beneath, and heaven above
Trembled at discovery of love.
Jesus was sitting in Moses' chair;
They brought the trembling woman there.
Moses commands she be stoned to death:
What was the sound of Jesus' breath?
He laid his hand on Moses' law:
The ancient heavens in silent **awe**,
Writ with curses from pole to pole,
All away began to roll:
The earth trembling and naked lay
In secret bed of mortal clay—

On Sinai fell the hand Divine
Putting back the bloody shrine—
And she heard the breath of God,
As she heard by Eden's flood :
" Good and evil are no more ;
Sinai's trumpets, cease to **roar** ;
Cease, finger of God, to write,
The heavens are not clean in thy sight.
Thou art good, and thou alone ;
Nor may the sinner cast one stone.
To be good only, **is** to be
A God, or else a Pharisee.
Thou Angel of the Presence Divine,
Thou didst create this body of mine,
Wherefore hast thou writ these laws
And created hell's dark jaws ?
My Power I will **take** from thee ;
A cold leper thou shalt be.
Though thou wast so pure and bright
That heaven was impure in thy sight,
Though thine oath turned heaven pale,
Though thy covenant built hell's gaol,
Though thou didst all to chaos roll
With the serpent for its soul,
Still the breath Divine does move,
And the breath Divine is love.
Mary, fear not.   Let me see
The seven devils that torment thee.
Hide not from my sight thy sin,
That forgiveness thou mayst win.

Hath no man condemned thee?"
"No man, Lord." "Then what is he
Who shall accuse thee? Come ye forth,
Fallen fiends of heavenly birth
That have forgot your ancient love,
And driven away my trembling dove:
You shall bow before her feet;
You shall lick the dust for meat;
And though you cannot love, but hate,
Shall be beggars at love's gate.
What was thy love? Let me see't:
Was it love or dark deceit?"
"Love too long from me has fled:
'Twas dark deceit, to earn my bread;
'Twas covet, or 'twas custom, or
Some trifle not worth caring for:
That these may call a shame and sin
Love's temple that God dwelleth in,
And hide in secret hidden shrine
The naked human form divine,
And render that a lawless thing
On which the soul expands her wing:
But this, O Lord, this was my sin—
When first I let these devils in,
In dark pretence to chastity
Blaspheming love, blaspheming thee.
Thence rose secret adulteries,
And thence did covet also rise.
My sin thou hast forgiven me;
Canst thou forgive my blasphemy?

Canst thou return to this dark hell
And in my burning bosom dwell?
And canst thou die that I may live?
And canst thou pity and forgive?"

THE GREY MONK.

I SEE, I see," the Mother said,
  " My children die for lack of bread!
What more has the merciless tyrant said?"
The Monk sat him down on her stony bed.

The blood red ran from the Grey Monk's side,
His hands and feet were wounded wide,
His body bent, his arms and knees
Like to the roots of ancient trees.

His eye was dry, no **tear** could **flow,**
A hollow groan **bespoke** his **woe ;**
He trembled and shuddered upon the bed ;
At length with a feeble cry he said :

" When God commanded this hand to write
In the shadowy hours of deep midnight,
He told me that all I wrote should prove
The bane of all that on earth I love.

" **My** brother starved between two walls,
His children's cry my soul appals—
I mocked at the rack and the grinding chain—
My bent body mocks at their torturing pain.

"Thy father drew his sword in the north,
With his thousands strong he is marched forth.
Thy brother hath armed himself in steel,
To revenge the wrongs thy children feel.

"But vain the sword, and vain the bow,—
They never can work war's overthrow;
The hermit's prayer and the widow's tear
Alone can free the world from fear.

"For a tear is an intellectual thing,
And a sigh is the sword of an angel king;
And the bitter groan of a martyr's woe
Is an arrow from the Almighty's bow."

The hand of vengeance found the bed
To which the purple tyrant fled;
The iron hand crushed the tyrant's head,
And became a tyrant in his stead.

SCOFFERS.

MOCK on, mock on, Voltaire, Rousseau,
　　Mock on, mock on; 'tis all in vain;
You throw the sand against the wind,
　And the wind blows it back again.

And every sand becomes a gem
　Reflected in the beams divine;
Blown back, they blind the mocking eye,
　But still in Israel's paths they shine.

The atoms of Democritus
  And Newton's particles of light
Are sands upon the Red Sea shore,
  Where Israel's tents do shine so bright.

THE TWO SONGS.

I HEARD an Angel singing,
  When the day was springing,
" Mercy, pity, and peace,
Are the world's release."

So he sang all day
Over the new-mown hay,
Till **the** sun went down,
And haycocks looked brown.

I heard a devil curse
Over the heath and the furse :
" Mercy could be no more
If there were nobody poor,
And pity no **more** could be
If all were happy as ye :
And mutual fear brings peace.
Misery's increase
Are mercy, pity, peace."

At his **curse** the sun went down,
And the heavens gave a frown.

THE WILD FLOWER'S SONG.

AS I wandered in the forest
   The green leaves among,
I heard a wild flower
   Singing a song.

" I slept in the earth
   In the silent night ;
I murmured my thoughts,
   And I felt delight.

" In the morning I went,
   As rosy as morn,
To seek for new joy,
   But I met with scorn."

MARY.

SWEET Mary, the first time she ever was
   there,
Came into the ball-room among the fair ;
The young men and maidens around her
   throng,
And these are the words upon every tongue :

" An angel is here from the heavenly climes,
Or again return the golden times ;

Her eyes outshine every brilliant ray,
She opens her lips—'tis the month of May."

Mary moves in soft beauty and conscious
    delight,
To augment with sweet smiles all the joys of
    the night,
Nor once blushes to own to the rest of the fair
That sweet love and beauty are worthy our
    care.

In the morning the villagers rose with delight,
And repeated with pleasure the joys of the
    night,
And Mary arose among friends to be free,
But no friend from henceforward thou, Mary,
    shalt see.

Some said she was proud, some called her a
    whore,
And some when she passed by shut-to the door;
A damp cold came o'er her, her blushes all
    fled,
Her lilies and roses are blighted and shed.

"Oh, why was I born with a different face?
Why was I not born like this envious race?
Why did Heaven adorn me with bountiful
    hand,
And then set me down in an envious land?

"To be weak as a lamb and smooth as a dove,
And not to raise envy, is called Christian love;
But, if you raise envy, your merit's to blame
For planting such spite in the weak and the
    tame.

"I will humble my beauty, I will not dress
    fine,
I will keep from the ball, and my eyes shall
    not shine;
And, if any girl's lover forsake her for me,
I'll refuse him my hand, and from envy go
    free."

She went out in the morning attired plain and
    neat;
"Proud Mary's gone mad," said the child in
    the street;
She went out in the morning in plain neat
    attire,
And came home in the evening bespattered
    with mire.

She trembled and wept, sitting on the bedside,
She forgot it was night, and she trembled and
    cried;
She forgot it was night, she forgot it was morn,
Her soft memory imprinted with faces of scorn;

With faces of scorn and with eyes of disdain,
Like foul fiends inhabiting Mary's mild brain;

She remembers no face like the human divine;
All faces have envy, sweet Mary, but thine.

And thine is the face of sweet love in despair,
And thine is the face of mild sorrow and care,
And thine is the face of wild terror and fear
That shall never be quiet till laid on its bier.

WILLIAM BOND.

I WONDER whether the girls are mad,
　　And I wonder whether they mean to kill,
And I wonder if William Bond will die,
　　For assuredly he is very ill.

He went to church on a May morning,
　　Attended by fairies one, two, and three;
But the angels of Providence drove them away,
　　And he returned home in misery.

He went not out to the field nor fold,
　　He went not out to the village nor town,
But he came home in a black, black cloud,
　　And took to his bed, and there lay down.

And an angel of Providence at his feet,
　　And an angel of Providence at his head,
And in the midst a black, black cloud,
　　And in the midst the sick man on his bed.

And on his right hand was Mary Green,
    And on his left hand was his sister Jane,
And their tears fell through the black, black
        cloud
    To drive away the sick man's pain.

' Oh, William, if thou dost another love,
    Dost another love better than poor Mary,
Go and take that other to be thy wife,
    And Mary Green shall her servant be."

" Yes, Mary, I do another love,
    Another I love far better than thee,
And another I will have for my wife :
    Then what have I to do with thee ?

" For thou art melancholy pale,
    And on thy head is the cold moon's shine,
But she is ruddy and bright as day,
    And the sunbeams dazzle from her eyne."

Mary trembled, and Mary chilled,
    And Mary fell down on the right-hand floor,
That William Bond and his sister Jane
    Scarce could recover Mary more.

When Mary woke and found her laid
    On the right hand of her William dear,
On the right hand of his loved bed,
    And saw her William Bond so near ;

The fairies that fled from William Bond
    Danced around her shining head ;
They danced over the pillow white,
    And the angels of Providence left the bed.

"I thought Love lived in the hot sunshine,
    But, oh, he lives in the moony light !
I thought to find Love in the heat of day,
    But sweet Love is the comforter of night.

"Seek Love in the pity of others' woe,
    In the gentle relief of another's care,
In the darkness of night and the winter's snow,
    With the naked and outcast—seek Love
      there."

IN A MYRTLE SHADE.

TO a lovely myrtle bound,
    Blossoms showering all round,
Oh, how weak and weary I
Underneath my myrtle lie !

Why should I be bound to thee,
O my lovely myrtle-tree ?
Love, free love, cannot be bound
To any tree that grows on ground.

YOUNG LOVE.

ARE not the joys of morning sweeter
   Than the joys of night?
And are the vigorous joys of youth
   Ashamed of the light?

Let age and sickness silent rob
   The vineyard in the night;
But those who burn with vigorous youth
   Pluck fruits before the light.

CUPID.

WHY was Cupid a boy?
   And why a boy was he?
He should have been a girl,
   For aught that I can see.

For he shoots with his bow,
   And the girl shoots with her eye;
And they both are merry and glad,
   And laugh when we do cry.

Then to make Cupid a boy
  Was surely a woman's plan,
For a boy never learns so much
  Till he has become a **man.**

And then he's so pierced with **cares,**
  And wounded with arrowy smarts,
That the whole business of his life
  Is to pick **out the** heads of the darts.

LOVE'S SECRET.

NEVER seek to tell thy love,
  Love that never told can be ;
For the gentle wind doth move
  Silently, invisibly.

I told my love, I told my love,
  I told her all my heart,
Trembling, cold, in ghastly fears.
  Ah ! she did depart !

Soon after she was gone from me,
  A traveller came by,
Silently, invisibly :
  He took her with a sigh.

THE SONG OF PHŒBE AND JELLICOE.

PHŒBE dressed like beauty's Queen,
    Jellicoe in faint pea-green ;
Sitting all beneath a grot
Where the little lambkins trot.

Maidens dancing, loves a-sporting,
All the country folks a-courting,
Susan, Johnny, Bab, and Joe,
Lightly tripping on a row.

Happy people, who can be
In happiness compared with ye ?
The Pilgrim with his crook and hat
Sees your happiness complete.

THE BIRDS.

He. WHERE thou dwellest, in what grove,
        Tell me, fair one, tell me, love ;
Where thou thy charming nest dost build,
    O thou pride of every field !

She. Yonder stands a lonely tree ;
        There I live and mourn for thee.
Morning drinks my silent tear,
    And evening winds my sorrow bear.

He. O thou summer's harmony,
    I have lived and mourned for thee ;
Each day I moan along the wood,
    And night hath heard my sorrows loud.

She. Dost thou truly long for me ?
    And am I thus sweet to thee ?
Sorrow now is **at an end,**
    O my lover and my friend !

He. Come ! on wings of joy we'll fly
To where my bower is hung on high ;
Come, and make thy calm retreat
Among green leaves **and** blossoms sweet.

THE LAND OF DREAMS.

AWAKE, awake, my little boy !
    Thou wast thy mother's only joy.
Why dost thou weep in thy gentle sleep ?
Oh, wake ! thy father doth thee keep."

" Oh, what land is the land of dreams ?
What are its mountains and what are its
    streams ?
Oh, father ! I saw my mother there,
Among the lilies by waters fair. ,

"Among the lambs clothed in white
She walked with her Thomas in sweet delight.

K

I wept for joy, like a dove I mourn,—
Oh, when shall I again return ?"

" Dear child ! I also by pleasant streams
Have wandered all night in the land of dreams ;
But, though calm and warm the waters wide,
I could not get to the other side."

" Father, O father ! what do we hear,
In this land of unbelief and fear ?
The land of dreams is better far,
Above the light of the morning star."

NIGHT AND DAY.

SILENT, silent night,
    Quench the holy light
Of thy torches bright :

For, possessed of Day,
Thousand spirits stray
That sweet joys betray.

Why should joys be sweet
Used with deceit,
Nor with sorrows meet ?

But an honest joy
Doth itself destroy
For a harlot coy.

FRAGMENTS.

H E who bends to himself a joy
    Does the winged life destroy ;
But **he** who kisses **the joy** as it flies
Lives in eternity's sunrise.

ABSTINENCE sows sand all over
    The ruddy limbs and flaming hair ;
But desire gratified
    Plants fruits of life and beauty there.

I **WALKED** abroad on a snowy day,
I asked **the soft snow with** me to play ;
She played and she melted in all her prime ;
And the winter called it a dreadful crime.

GREAT **things are** done when men and moun-
    tains meet ;
These are not done by jostling in the street.

SINCE all the riches of this world
    May be gifts from the devil and earthly
    kings,
I should suspect that I worshipped the **devil**
    If **I thanked my** God for worldly things.

ALL pictures that's painted with sense or with
    thought
Are painted by madmen, as sure as a groat.
For the greater the fool, in the Art the more
    blest,
And when they are drunk they always paint
    best.
They never can Raphael it, Fuseli it, or Blake
    it :
If they can't see an outline, pray how can they
    make it?
All men have drawn outlines whenever they
    saw them ;
Madmen see outlines, and therefore they draw
    them.

THE sword sang on the barren heath,
    The sickle in the fruitful field ;
The sword he sang a song of death,
    But could not make the sickle yield.

THE Angel that presided o'er my birth
Said : "Little Creature, formed of joy and
    mirth,
Go, live without the help of anything on earth.'

THE MARRIAGE OF HEAVEN AND HELL.

(1790.)

THE MARRIAGE OF HEAVEN
AND HELL.

(1790.)

THE ARGUMENT.

RINTRAH roars and shakes his fires in the
    burdened air;
Hungry clouds swag on the deep.

Once meek, and in a perilous path,
The just man kept his course along
The vale of death.
Roses **are** planted where thorns grow,
And on the barren heath
Sing the honey bees.

Then the perilous path was planted:
And **a** river and a spring
On every cliff and tomb:
And on the bleached bones
Red clay brought forth.

Till the villain left the paths **of case**
To walk in perilous paths, and drive
The just man into barren climes.

Now the sneaking serpent walks
In mild humility :
And the just man rages in the wilds
Where lions roam.

Rintrah roars and shakes his fires in the
    burdened air,
Hungry clouds swag on the deep.

As a new heaven is begun, and it is now thirty-three years since its advent, the Eternal Hell revives. And lo ! Swedenborg is the Angel sitting at the tomb : his writings are the linen clothes folded up. Now is the dominion of Edom, and the return of Adam into Paradise : see Isaiah, xxxiv. and xxxv. chapters.

Without contraries is no progression. Attraction and Repulsion, Reason and Energy, Love and Hate, are necessary to Human existence.

From these contraries spring what the religious call Good and Evil. Good is the Passive that obeys Reason. Evil is the Active springing from Energy.

Good is Heaven. Evil is Hell.

The Voice of the Devil.

All Bibles or sacred codes have been the causes of the following Errors :—

1. That man has two real existing principles, viz., a Body and a Soul.
2. That Energy, called Evil, is alone from the Body : and that Reason, called Good, is alone from the Soul.
3. That God will torment Man in Eternity for following his Energies.

But the following Contraries to these are true :—

1. Man has no Body distinct from his Soul, for that called Body is a portion of Soul discerned by the five Senses, the chief inlets of Soul in this age.
2. Energy is the only life, and is from the Body : and Reason is the bound or outward circumference of Energy.
3. Energy is Eternal Delight.

Those who restrain desire, do so because theirs is weak enough to be restrained ; and the restrainer, or reason, usurps its place, and governs the unwilling.

And being restrained, it by degrees becomes passive, till it is only the shadow of desire.

The history of this is written in Paradise Lost, and the Governor or Reason is called Messiah.

And the original Archangel or possessor of he command of the heavenly host, is called the Devil or Satan, and his children are called Sin and Death.

But in the book of Job, Milton's Messiah is called Satan.

For this history has been adopted by both parties.

It indeed appeared to Reason as if Desire was cast out : but the Devil's account is, that the Messiah fell, and formed a heaven of what he stole from the Abyss.

This is shown in the Gospel, where he prays to the Father to send the Comforter, or Desire, that Reason may have ideas to build on : the Jehovah of the Bible being no other than he who dwells in flaming fire.

Know that after Christ's death he became Jehovah.

But in Milton, the Father is Destiny, the Son a Ratio of the five senses, and the Holy Ghost Vacuum !

Note.—The reason Milton wrote in fetters when he wrote of Angels and God, and at liberty when of Devils and Hell, is because he was a true Poet, and of the Devil's party without knowing it.

A Memorable Fancy.

As I was walking among **the** fires of **hell,** delighted with the enjoyments of Genius, which to Angels look like torments and **in-**sanity, I collected some of their Proverbs : thinking that **as** the sayings used in a nation mark its character, so the Proverbs of Hell show the nature of Infernal wisdom better than any description **of** buildings or garments.

When I came home, **on** the abyss of the five senses, where a flat-sided steep frowns over the present world, I saw a mighty Devil folded in black clouds, hovering on the sides of the rock : with corroding fires he wrote the following sentence, **now** perceived by **the** minds of men, and read by them on earth.

How do you know but every bird that **cuts** the airy way, is an immense world of delight, closed by your senses five ?

Proverbs of Hell.

In seed time learn, in harvest teach, in winter enjoy.

Drive your cart and your plough over the bones of the dead.

The road of excess leads to the palace of wisdom.

Prudence is a rich ugly old maid courted by
Incapacity.

He who desires but acts not, breeds pestilence.

The cut worm forgives the plough.

Dip him in the river who loves water.

A fool sees not the same tree that a wise
man sees.

He whose face gives no light shall never
become a star.

Eternity is in love with the productions of
time.

The busy bee has no time for sorrow.

The hours of folly are measured by the clock :
but of wisdom no clock can measure.

All wholesome food is caught without a net
or a trap.

Bring out number, weight, and measure in
a year of dearth.

No bird soars too high if he soars with his
own wings.

A dead body revenges not injuries.

The most sublime act is to set another
before you.

If the fool would persist in his folly he would
become wise.

Folly is the cloak of knavery.

Shame is Pride's cloak.

Prisons are built with stones of Law,
Brothels with bricks of Religion.

The pride of the peacock is the glory of God.

The lust of the goat is the bounty of God.

The wrath of the lion is the wisdom of God.

The nakedness of woman is the work of God.

Excess of sorrow laughs. Excess of **joy** weeps.

The roaring of lions, the howling of wolves, **the** raging of **the** stormy sea, and the destructive sword are portions of eter-**nity** too great for the eye of man.

The fox condemns the trap, not himself.

Joys impregnate. Sorrows bring forth.

Let man wear the fell of the lion, woman the fleece of the sheep.

The bird a nest, the spider a web, **man** friendship.

The **selfish** smiling fool, and the **sullen** frowning fool shall both be thought wise, that they may be a rod.

What is now proved was once only imagined.

The rat, the mouse, the fox, the rabbit, watch the roots ; the lion, the tiger, **the** horse, the elephant, watch the fruits.

The cistern contains : the fountain overflows.

One thought fills immensity.

Always be ready to speak your mind, and **a** base man will avoid you.

Everything possible to be believed is an image of truth.

The eagle never lost so much time, as when
  he submitted to learn of the crow.

The fox provides for himself : but God provides for the lion.

Think in the morning. Act in the noon. Eat
  in the evening. Sleep in the night.

He who has suffered you to impose on him
  knows you.

As the plough follows words, so does God
  reward prayers.

The tigers of wrath are wiser than the horses
  of instruction.

Expect poison from the standing water.

You never know what is enough unless you
  know what is more than enough.

Listen to the fool's reproach ! it is a kingly
  title !

The eyes of fire, the nostrils of air, the
  mouth of water, the beard of earth.

The weak in courage is strong in cunning.

The apple tree never asks the beech how he
  shall grow ; nor the lion the horse how
  he shall take his prey.

The thankful receiver bears a plentiful
  harvest.

If others had not been foolish, we should be so.

The soul of sweet delight can never be
  defiled.

When thou seest an Eagle thou seest a portion of Genius, lift up thy head !

As the caterpillar chooses the fairest leaves to lay her eggs on, so the priest lays his curse on the fairest joys.

To create **a** little flower is the **labour of** ages.

Damn braces : Bless relaxes.

The best wine is the oldest, the best **water** the newest.

Prayers plough not ! Praises reap not !

Joys laugh **not** ! Sorrows weep not !

The head Sublime, the heart Pathos, the genitals Beauty, the hands and feet Proportion.

As the air to a bird or the sea to a fish, so is contempt to the contemptible.

The crow wished everything was black, **the owl** that everything was **white.**

Exuberance is Beauty.

If the lion was advised by the fox he would be cunning.

Improvement makes straight roads, but the crooked roads without Improvement **are** roads of Genius.

Sooner murder an infant in its cradle than nurse unacted desires.

Where man is not nature is barren.

Truth can never be told so as to be understood and not be believed.

Enough ! **or Too** much.

The ancient Poets animated all sensible objects with Gods or Geniuses, calling them by the names and adorning them with the properties of woods, rivers, mountains, lakes, cities, nations, and whatever their enlarged **and numerous** senses could perceive.

And particularly they studied the genius of **each city and country,** placing it under **its** mental deity.

Till a system was formed which some **took** advantage of, and enslaved the vulgar by attempting to realise or abstract the mental deities from their objects ; thus began Priesthood. Choosing forms of worship from poetic tales.

And at length they pronounced that the Gods had ordered such things.

Thus man **forgot** that all deities reside in the human breast.

A Memorable Fancy.

The Prophets Isaiah and Ezekiel dined with **me, and I** asked them **how they dared so** roundly **to** assert that **God** spake to them ; and whether they did not think at the time that they would be misunderstood, and so be the cause of imposition.

Isaiah answered : I saw no God, nor heard

any in a finite organical perception : but my senses discovered the infinite in everything : and as I was then persuaded, and remain confirmed that the voice of honest indignation is the voice of God, I cared not for consequences, but **wrote**.

Then I asked : Does a firm persuasion that a thing is so, make it so?

He replied : All poets believe that **it** does, and in ages of imagination this firm persuasion removed mountains : but many are not capable of a firm persuasion of anything.

Then Ezekiel said : The philosophy of the east taught the first principles of human perception ; some nations **held one principle** for the origin, and some another : **we of** Israel taught that the Poetic Genius (as you now call it) was the first principle, and all the others merely derivative, which was the cause of our despising the Priests and Philosophers of other countries, and prophesying that all **Gods** would at last be proved to originate in ours, and **to** be tributaries of the Poetic Genius ; it was this that our great poet King David desired so fervently, and invokes so pathetically, saying by this he conquers enemies and governs Kingdoms ; and **we** so loved our God, that we cursed in his name all the deities of surrounding nations, and asserted that they had rebelled : from these opinions the vulgar came to think that all nations would at last be subject to the Jews.

This, said he, like all firm persuasions, is come to pass, for all nations believe the Jew's code and worship the Jew's god, and what greater subjection can be?

I heard this with some wonder, and must confess my own conviction. After dinner I asked Isaiah to favour the world with his lost works: he said none of equal value was lost; Ezekiel said the same of his.

I also asked Isaiah what made him go naked and bare-foot three years. He answered, The same that made our friend Diogenes the Grecian.

I then asked Ezekiel why he ate dung, and lay so long on his right and left side? He answered, The desire of raising other men into a perception of the infinite; this the North American tribes practise; and is he honest who resists his genius or conscience, only for the sake of present ease or gratification?

The ancient tradition that the world will be consumed in fire at the end of six thousand years is true, as I have heard from Hell.

For the cherub with his flaming sword is hereby commanded to leave his guard at tree of life; and when he does, the whole creation will be consumed, and appear infinite and holy, whereas it now appears finite and corrupt.

This will come to pass by an improvement of sensual enjoyment.

But first the notion that man has a body distinct from his soul is to be expunged : this I shall do by printing **in the** infernal method by corrosives, which in Hell are salutary, and medicinal, melting apparent surfaces away, and displaying the infinite which was hid.

If the doors of perception were cleansed, everything would appear to man as it is, infinite.

For man has closed himself up, till he sees all things through narrow chinks of his cavern.

A Memorable Fancy.

I was in a Printing-house in Hell, and saw the method in which knowledge is transmitted from generation to generation.

In the first chamber was a Dragon Man, clearing away the rubbish from **a** cave's mouth ; within a number of Dragons were hollowing the cave.

In the second chamber was **a** Viper, folding round the rock and the cave, and others adorning it with gold, silver, and precious stones.

In the third chamber was an Eagle, with

wings and feathers of air: he caused the inside of the cave to be infinite: around were numbers of Eagle-like men, who built palaces in the immense cliffs.

In the fourth chamber were Lions of flaming fire raging around, and melting the metals into livid fluids.

In the fifth chamber were Unnamed forms, which cast the metals into the expanse.

There they were received by Men, who occupied the sixth chamber, and took the forms of books, and were arranged in libraries.

The Giants who formed this world into its sensual existence, and now seem to live in it in chains, are in truth the causes of its life and the sources of all activity ; but the chains are the cunning of weak and tame minds, which have power to resist energy, according to the proverb, the weak in courage is strong in cunning.

Thus one portion of being is the Prolific, the other, the Devouring : to the devourer it seems as if the producer was in his chains, but it is not so ; he only takes portions of existence, and fancies that the whole.

But the Prolific would cease to be Prolific unless the Devourer, as a sea, received the excess of his delights.

Some will say, Is not God alone the Prolific ?

I answer, God only Acts and Is in existing beings or Men.

These two classes of men are always upon earth, and they should be enemies ; whoever tries to reconcile them seeks to destroy existence. Religion is an endeavour to reconcile the two.

Note.—Jesus Christ did not wish to unite but to separate them, as in the Parable of sheep and goats ! and he says, I came not to send Peace, but a Sword.

Messiah, or Satan, or Tempter was formerly thought to be one of the Antediluvians, who are our Energies.

A Memorable Fancy.

An Angel came to me and said, O pitiable foolish young man ! O horrible ! O dreadful state ! Consider the hot burning dungeon thou art preparing for thyself to all eternity, to which thou art going in such career.

I said, Perhaps you will be willing to show me my eternal lot, and we will contemplate together upon it, and see whether your lot or mine is most desirable.

So he took me through a stable, and through a church, and down into the church vault, at the end of which was a mill : through the mill

we went, and came to a cave ; down the wind-
ing cavern we groped our tedious way, till a
void, boundless as a nether sky, appeared
beneath us, and we held by the roots of trees
and hung over this immensity : but I said, If
you please we will commit ourselves to this
void, and see whether providence is here also.
If you will not, I will.   But he answered, Do
not presume, O young man ; but as we here
remain, behold thy lot, which will soon appear
when the darkness passes away.

So I remained with him, sitting in the
twisted root of an oak ; he was suspended in
a fungus, which hung with the head downward
into the deep.

By degrees we beheld the infinite Abyss,
fiery as the smoke of a burning city : beneath
us at an immense distance was the sun, black
but shining ; round it were fiery tracks on
which revolved vast spiders crawling after
their prey, which flew, or rather swum, in the
infinite deep, in the most terrific shapes of
animals sprung from corruption ; and the air
was full of them, and seemed composed of
them ; these are Devils, and called Powers
of the air.   I now asked my companion which
was my eternal lot ?   He said between the
black and white spiders.

But now, from between the black and white
spiders a cloud and fire burst and rolled

through the deep, blackening all beneath, so that the nether deep grew black as a sea, and rolled with a terrible noise : beneath us was nothing now to be seen but a black tempest, till looking east between the clouds and the waves, we saw a cataract of blood mixed with fire, and not many stones-throw from us appeared and sunk again the scaly fold of a monstrous serpent : at last to the east, distant about three degrees, appeared a fiery crest above the waves, slowly it reared like a ridge of golden rocks till we discovered two globes of crimson fire, from which the sea fled away in clouds of smoke, and now we saw it was the head of Leviathan ; his forehead was divided into streaks of green and purple, like those on a tiger's forehead ; soon we saw his mouth and red gills hang just above the raging foam, tinging the black deep with beams of blood, advancing toward us with all the fury of a spiritual existence.

My friend the Angel climbed up from his station into the mill ; I remained alone, and then this appearance was no more, but I found myself sitting on a pleasant bank beside a river by moonlight hearing a harper who sung to the harp, and his theme was, The man who never alters his opinion is like standing water, and breeds reptiles of the mind.

But I arose and sought for the mill, and

there I found my Angel who, surprised, asked me how I escaped?

I answered, All that we saw was owing to your metaphysics : for when you ran away, I found myself on a bank by moonlight hearing a harper.   But now we have seen my eternal lot, shall I show you yours?   He laughed at my proposal : but I by force suddenly caught him in my arms, and flew westerly through the night, till we were elevated above the earth's shadow ; then I flung myself with him directly into the body of the sun ; here I clothed myself in white, and taking in my hand Swedenborg's volumes, sunk from the glorious clime, and passed all the planets till we came to Saturn ; here I stayed to rest and then leapt into the void between Saturn and the fixed stars.

Here, said I, is your lot, in this space, if space it may be called.   Soon we saw the stable and the church, and I took him to the altar and opened the Bible, and lo ! it was a deep pit into which I descended, driving the Angel before me ; soon we saw seven houses of brick, one we entered ; in it were a number of monkeys, baboons, and all of that species chained by the middle, grinning and snatching at one another, but withheld by the shortness of their chains ; however, I saw that they sometimes grew numerous, and then the weak were caught by the strong, and with a grinning aspect, first coupled with and then devoured, by plucking off first one limb and then another till the body was left a helpless trunk, this, after grinning and kissing it with seeming fondness, they devoured too ; and here and there I saw one savourily picking the flesh off of his own tail : As the stench terribly annoyed us both, we went into the mill, and I in my hand brought the skeleton of a body which in the mill was Aristotle's "Analytics."

So the Angel said : Thy phantasy has imposed upon me, and thou oughtest to be ashamed.

I answered : We impose on one another, and it is but lost time to converse with you whose works are only Analytics.

I have always found that Angels have the vanity to speak of themselves as the only wise : this they do with a confident insolence sprouting from systematic reasoning.

Thus Swedenborg boasts of what he writes is new ; though it is only the Contents or Index of already published books.

A man carried a monkey about **for a** show, and because he was a little wiser than the monkey, grew vain and conceived himself as much wiser than seven men. It is so with Swedenborg ; he shows the folly of churches and exposes hypocrites, till he imagines that all are religious, and himself the single one on earth that ever broke a net.

Now hear a plain fact : Swedenborg has not written one new truth.

Now hear another : he has written all the old falsehoods.

And now hear the reason. He conversed with Angels who are all religious, and conversed not with Devils who all hate religion, for he was incapable through his conceited notions.

Thus Swedenborg's writings are a recapitulation of all superficial opinions, and an analysis of the more sublime, but no further.

Have now another plain fact. Any man of mechanical talents may, from the writings of Paracelsus or Jacob Behmen, produce ten thousand volumes of equal value with Swedenborg's ; and from those of Dante or Shakespear, an infinite number.

But when he has done this, let him not say that he knows better than his master, for he only holds a candle in sunshine.

A Memorable Fancy.

Once I saw a Devil in a flame of fire, who arose before an Angel that sat on a cloud, and the Devil uttered these words :—

The worship of God is, Honouring his gifts in other men each according to his genius,

and loving the greatest men best : those who
envy or calumniate great men hate God, for
there is no other God.

The Angel hearing this became almost blue,
but mastering himself he grew yellow, and at
last white pink and smiling, and then replied,

Thou Idolater, is not God One? and is not
he visible in Jesus Christ? and has not Jesus
Christ given his sanction to the law of ten
commandments? and are not all other men
fools, sinners, and nothings?

The Devil answered : Bray a fool in a
mortar with wheat, yet shall not his folly be
beaten out of him : if Jesus Christ is the
greatest man, you ought to love him in the
greatest degree ; now hear how he has given
his sanction to the law of ten commandments :
did he not mock at the Sabbath, and so mock
at the Sabbath's God? murder those who were
murdered because of him? turn away the law
from the woman taken in adultery? steal the
labour of others to support him? bear false
witness when he omitted making a defence
before Pilate? covet when he prayed for
his disciples, and when he bid them shake
off the dust of their feet against such as
refused to lodge them? I tell you no virtue
can exist without breaking these ten commandments : Jesus was all virtue, and acted
from impulse, not from rules.

When he had so spoken, I beheld the Angel who stretched out his arms embracing the flame of fire, and he was consumed and arose as Elijah.

Note.—This Angel, who is now become a Devil, is my particular friend: we often read the Bible together in its infernal or diabolical sense, which the world shall have if they behave well.

I have also the Bible of Hell, which the world shall have whether they will or no.

One law for the Lion and Ox is Oppression.

A SONG OF LIBERTY.

1. The Eternal Female groaned! it was heard over all the Earth :
2. Albion's coast is sick silent ; the American meadows faint !
3. Shadows of Prophecy shiver along by the lakes and the rivers, and mutter across the ocean.   France, rend down thy dungeon.
4. Golden Spain, burst the barriers of old Rome ;
5. Cast thy keys, O Rome, into the deep down falling, even to eternity down falling,
6. And weep.

7. In her trembling hands she took the new-born terror howling ;

8. On those infinite mountains of light, **now** barred out by the Atlantic sea, the new-born fire stood before the starry king :

9. Flagged with grey-browed snows and thunderous visages the jealous wings waved over the deep.

10. The speary hand burned aloft, unbuckled was the shield, forth went the hand of jealousy among the flaming hair, and hurled the new-born wonder through the starry night.

11. The fire, the fire is falling !

12. Look up ! look up ! O citizen of London, enlarge thy countenance : O Jew, **leave** counting gold ! return to **thy oil and** wine ; O African ! black African ! (go, winged thought, widen his forehead).

13. The fiery limbs, the flaming hair, shot like the sinking sun into the western sea.

14. Waked from his eternal sleep, the hoary element roaring fled away ;

15. Down rushed, beating his wings in vain, the jealous king ; his grey - browed counsellors, thunderous warriors, curled veterans, among helms, and shields, **and** chariots, horses, elephants, banners, **castles,** slings, and rocks,

16. Falling, rushing, ruining ! buried in the ruins on Urthona's dens.

17. All night beneath the ruins, then their sullen flames faded emerge round the gloomy king,

18. With thunder and fire ; leading his starry hosts through the waste wilderness, he promulgates his ten commands, glancing his beamy eyelids over the deep in dark dismay,

19. Where the son of fire in his eastern cloud, while the morning plumes her golden breast,

20. Spurning the clouds written with curses, stamps the stony law to dust, loosing the eternal horses from the dens of night, crying, *EMPIRE IS NO MORE! AND NOW THE LION AND WOLF SHALL CEASE.*

Chorus.

Let the Priests of the Raven of dawn no longer in deadly black with hoarse note curse the sons of joy. Nor his accepted brethren, whom, tyrant, he calls free, lay the bound or build the roof. Nor pale religious letchery call that virginity, that wishes but acts not !

For everything that lives is Holy.

THERE IS NO

NATURAL RELIGION.

THE ARGUMENT.

MAN has no notion of moral fitness but *can be intuitive* from Education.

Naturally **he** is only a natural organ, subject to Sense.

I.

Man's perceptions are not bounded by organs of perception : he perceives more than sense (though ever so acute) can discover.

positively deductive of the chief

II.

Man by his reasoning power can only compare and judge of what he has already perceived.

III.

From a perception of only three senses, or three elements, none can deduce a fourth or fifth.

IV.

None could have other than natural **or organic** thoughts if he had none but organic perceptions.

V.

Man's desires are limited by his perceptions : none can detect what he has not perceived.

VI.

The desires and perceptions of man, untaught by anything but organs of sense, must be limited to objects of sense.

I.

Man cannot naturally perceive, but through his natural or bodily organs.

II.

Reason, or the ratio of all we have already known, is not the same that it shall be when we know more.

Therefore,

God becomes as we are, that we may be as he is.

EXTRACTS FROM THE PROPHETIC BOOKS.

M

VISIONS OF THE DAUGHTERS
OF ALBION.

(1793.)

THE village dog
    Barks at the breaking day ; the nightin-
    gale has done lamenting ;
The lark does rustle in the ripe corn, and the
    Eagle returns
From nightly prey and lifts his golden beak
    to the pure east :
Shaking the dust from his immortal pinions,
    to awake
The sun that sleeps too long. Arise, my
    Theotormon, I am pure
Because the night is gone that closed me in
    its deadly black.
They told me that the night and day were all
    I could see :
They told me that I had five senses to enclose
    me up,
And they enclosed my infinite brain into a
    narrow circle,

And sank my heart into the abyss, a red round
   globe hot-burning,
Till all from life I was obliterated and erased.

.   .   .   .   .   .

With what sense is it that the chicken shuns
   the ravenous hawk?
With what sense does the tame pigeon mea-
   sure out the expanse?
With what sense does the bee form cells?
   Have not the mouse and frog
Eyes and ears and sense of touch? yet are
   their habitations
And their pursuits as different as their forms
   and as their joys.
Ask the wild ass why he refuses burdens, and
   the meek camel
Why he loves man : is it because of eye, ear,
   mouth or skin,
Or breathing nostrils? No : for these the
   wolf and tiger have.
Ask the blind worm the secrets of the grave
   and why her spires
Love to curl around the bones of death : and
   ask the ravenous snake
Where she gets her poison : and the winged
   eagle why he loves the sun :
And then tell me the thoughts of man, that
   have been hid of old.

.   .   .   .   .   .

Tell me what is the night or day to one over-
    flowed with woe?
Tell me what is a thought? and of what sub-
    stance is it made?
Tell me what is a joy? and in what garden do
    joys grow?
And in what river swim the sorrows? and upon
    what mountains
Wave shadows **of** discontent? **and** in what
    houses dwell the wretched,
Drunken with woe forgotten, and shut up from
    cold despair?

Tell me where dwell the thoughts forgotten
    till thou call them forth?
Tell me where dwell the joys of old? and
    where the ancient loves?
And when will they renew again, and the night
    of oblivion be past?
That I might traverse times and spaces far
    remote and bring
Comforts into a present sorrow **and a** night
    of **pain**!
Where goest thou, O thought? to what remote
    land is thy flight?
If thou returnest to the present moment of
    affliction,
Wilt thou bring comforts on thy wings, and
    dews and honey and balm,

Or poison from the desert wilds, from the eyes
    of the envier?

   .   .   .   .   .   .

Does not the great mouth laugh at a gift? and
    the narrow eyelids mock
At the labour that is above payment? and wilt
    thou take the ape
For thy counsellor or the dog for a school-
    master to thy children?
Does he who contemns poverty, and he who
    turns with abhorrence
From usury feel the same passion, or are they
    moved alike?

   .   .   .   .   .   .

Does the whale worship at thy footsteps as the
    hungry dog?
Or does he scent the mountain prey because
    his nostrils wide
Draw in the ocean? Does his eye discern the
    flying cloud
As the raven's eye? or does he measure the
    expanse like the vulture?
Does the still spider view the cliffs where the
    eagles hide their young?
Or does the fly rejoice because the harvest is
    brought in?
Does not the eagle scorn the earth, and
    despise the treasures beneath?
But the mole knoweth what is there, and the
    worm shall tell it thee.

Does not the worm erect a pillar in the
    mouldering churchyard,
And a palace of eternity in the jaws **of the**
    hungry grave?
Over his porch these words are written:
    " Take thy bliss, O man !
And sweet shall be thy taste, and sweet thy
    infant joys renew."

.   .   .   .   .   .

Does the sun walk in glorious raiment on the
    secret floor
Where the cold miser spreads his gold? or
    does the bright cloud drop
On his stone threshold? Does his eye behold
    the beam that brings
Expansion to the eye of pity? or will he bind
    himself
Beside the ox to thy hard furrow? . . .
The sea-fowl takes the wintry blast for a
    covering to her limbs:
And the wild snake the pestilence to adorn him
    with gems and gold.
And trees and birds and beasts and **man**
    behold their eternal joy.
Arise, little glancing wings, and sing your
    infant joy !
Arise and drink your bliss, for everything that
    lives is holy.

MILTON : A POEM (1804).

AND did those feet in ancient time
   Walk upon England's mountains green :
And was the holy Lamb of God
On England's pleasant pastures seen ?

And did the Countenance Divine
Shine forth upon our clouded hills ?
And was Jerusalem builded here,
Among these dark Satanic Mills ?

Bring me my Bow of burning gold :
Bring me my Arrows of desire :
Bring me my Spear : O clouds unfold :
Bring me my Chariot of fire !

I will not cease from Mental Fight,
Nor shall my Sword sleep in my hand :
Till we have built Jerusalem,
In England's green and pleasant Land.

   .   .   .   .   .   .

Los is by mortals named Time, Enitharmon
   is named Space ;
But they depict him bald and aged, who is
   eternal youth
All powerful, and his locks flourish like the
   brows of morning ;

He is the Spirit of Prophecy, the ever appa-
    rent Elias.
Time is the mercy of Eternity, without Time's
    swiftness,
Which is the swiftest of all things, all were
    eternal torment.

    .   .   .   .   .   .

This Wine-press is called War on earth ; it is
    the Printing-press
Of Los : and here he lays his words in order
    above the mortal brain,
As cogs are formed in a wheel to turn the cogs
    of the adverse wheel.

Timbrils and violins sport around the Wine-
    presses : the little Seed,
The sportive Root, the Earth-worm ; the gold
    Beetle ; the wise Emmet ;
Dance round the Wine-presses of Luvah : the
    centipede is there :
The ground Spider with many eyes : the Mole
    clothed in velvet :
The ambitious Spider in his sullen web : the
    lucky golden Spinner :
The Earwig armed : the tender Maggot, em-
    blem of immortality :
The Flea : Louse : Bug : the Tape-worm : all
    the armies of Disease,
Visible or invisible to the slothful vegetating
    man ;

The slow Slug : the Grasshopper that sings
    and laughs and drinks :
Winter comes, he folds his slender bones
    without a murmur.
The Cruel Scorpion is there ; the Gnat ;
    Wasp ; Hornet ; and the Honey Bee :
The Toad and venomous Newt : the Serpent
    clothed in gems and gold :
They throw off their gorgeous raiment : they
    rejoice with loud jubilee
Around the Wine-presses of Luvah, naked
    and drunk with wine.
There is the Nettle that stings with soft down ;
    and there
The indignant Thistle, whose bitterness is
    bred in his milk :
Who feeds on contempt of his neighbour :
    there all the idle Weeds,
That creep around the obscure places, show
    their various limbs,
Naked in all their beauty dancing round the
    Wine-presses.
But in the Wine-presses the Human grapes
    sing not nor dance.

.   .   .   .   .   .

They dance around the dying, and they drink
    the howl and groan ;
They catch the shrieks in cups of gold, they
    hand them to one another.

These are the sports of love, and these the
    sweet delights of amorous play—
Tears of the grape, the death-sweat of the
    cluster, the last sigh
Of the mild youth who listens to the luring
    songs of Luvah.

.   .   .   .   .   .

In Eternity the four Arts, Poetry, Painting,
    Music,
And Architecture which is Science, are the
    Four Faces of Man.
Not so in Time and Space: there three are
    shut out, and only
Science remains through Mercy: and by
    means of Science the Three
Became apparent in Time and Space in the
    three Professions:
Poetry in Religion: Music, Law: Painting in
    Physic and Surgery.
That man may live upon Earth till the time
    of his awakening.

.   .   .   .   .   .

The Sons of Los build Moments, and Minutes,
    and Hours,
And Days, and Months, and Years, and Ages,
    and Periods: wondrous buildings.
And every moment has a Couch of gold for
    soft repose
(A Moment equals a pulsation of the artery),

And between every two Moments stands a
    Daughter of Beulah
To feed the sleepers on their couches with
    maternal care.
And every Minute has an azure Tent with
    silken veils.
And every Hour has a bright golden Gate
    carved with skill.
And every Day and Night has Walls of brass
    and Gates of adamant,
Shining like precious stones, and ornamented
    with appropriate signs :
And every Month a silver paved Terrace
    builded high :
And every Year invulnerable Barriers with
    high Towers :
And every Age is Moated deep with Bridges
    of silver and gold !
And every Seven Ages is encircled with a
    Flaming Fire.
Now Seven Ages is amounting to Two Hun-
    dred Years,
Each has its Guard, each Moment, Minute,
    Hour, Day, Month, and Year.
All are the work of Fairy hands of the Four
    Elements,
The Guards are Angels of Providence on duty
    evermore.
Every Time less than a pulsation of the
    artery

Is equal in its period and value to Six Thousand Years,
For in this Period the Poet's Work is Done ;
 and all the Great
Events of Time start forth and are conceived
 in such a Period,
Within a moment : a Pulsation of the Artery.

The Sky is an immortal Tent, built by the
 Sons of Los :
And every Space that a man views around his
 dwelling-place,
Standing on his own roof, or in his garden on
 a mount
Twenty-five cubits in height, such **space** is his
 Universe ;
And on its verge the Sun rises and sets : **the**
 Clouds bow
To meet the flat Earth and the Sea in such
 an ordered Space :
The starry heavens reach no further, but here
 . **bend** and set
On all sides : and the two Poles turn on their
 valves of gold :
And if he move his dwelling-place, his heavens
 also move
Where'er he goes, and all his neighbourhood
 bewails his loss.

Thou hearest the Nightingale begin the Song
    of Spring :
The Lark sitting upon his **earthy** bed, just as
    the morn
Appears, listens silent : then springing **from**
    the waving Corn-field, loud
He leads the Choir of Day ; trill, trill, trill,
    trill :
Mounting upon the wings **of light into** the
    Great Expanse ;
Re-echoing against the lovely blue and shining
    heavenly Shell :
His little throat labours **with** inspiration ;
    every feather
On throat and breast and wings vibrates with
    the effluence Divine.
All Nature listens silent to him, and the awful
    Sun
Stands still upon the Mountain looking **on**
    this little Bird
With eyes of soft humility, and wonder, love,
    and awe.
Then loud from their green covert all the Birds
    begin their Song,
The Thrush, the Linnet, and the Goldfinch,
    Robin and the Wren
Awake the Sun from his sweet reverie upon
    the Mountain :
The Nightingale again assays **his** song, and
    through **the day**

And through the night warbles luxuriant :
    every Bird of Song
Attending his loud harmony with admiration
    and love.
This is a Vision of the lamentations of Beulah
    over Ololon.

Thou **perceivest** the Flowers put forth their
    precious Odours :
And none can tell how from so small a centre
    come such sweets ;
Forgetting that within that Centre Eternity
    expands
Its ever enduring doors, that Og and **Anak**
    fiercely guard.
First, ere the morning breaks, joy opens **in**
    the flowery bosoms,
Joy even to tears, which the Sun rising dries :
    first the Wild Thyme
And Meadow-sweet, downy and soft, waving
    among the reeds,
Light springing **on** the air lead the sweet
    Dance : they wake
The Honeysuckle sleeping on the Oak : the
    flaunting beauty
Revels along upon the wind : the White-thorn
    lovely May
Opens her many lovely eyes : listening the
    Rose still sleeps ;
None dare **to** wake her : soon she bursts her
    crimson-curtained **bed,**

And comes forth in the majesty of beauty : every Flower,

The Pink, the Jessamine, the Wall-flower, the Carnation,

The Jonquil, the mild Lily opes her heavens : every Tree

And Flower and Herb soon fill the air with an innumerable Dance,

Yet all in order sweet and lovely. Men are sick with Love.

Such is a Vision of the lamentation of Beulah over Ololon.

.　　.　　.　　.　　.　　.

Just at the place, to where the Lark mounts, is a Crystal Gate,

It is the entrance of the First Heaven named Luther ; for

The Lark is Los's Messenger through the Twenty-Seven Churches,

That the Seven Eyes of God who walk even to Satan's Seat

Through all the Twenty-Seven Churches, may not slumber nor sleep.

But the Lark's nest is at the Gate of Los : . . . and the Lark is Los's Messenger.

When on the highest lift of his light pinions he arrives

At that bright Gate, another Lark meets him, and back to back

They touch their pinion's tip and each de-
scend
To their respective Earths, and there all night
consult **with** Angels
Of Providence, and with the Eyes of God all
night **in** slumber
Inspired : and **at the** dawn of day send out
another Lark
Into another Heaven to carry news upon his
wings. . . .
Thus **to** Immortals the Lark is a mighty
Angel.

.   .   .   .   .   .

All that can be annihilated must be annihi-
lated,
That the children of Jerusalem may be saved
from slavery.
There is a Negation, and there is a Con-
trary :
The Negation must be destroyed to redeem
the Contraries.
The Negation is the Spectre : the Reasoning
Power in Man ;
This **is** a false Body : an Incrustation over my
Immortal
Spirit : a Selfhood which must be put off and
annihilated alway,
To cleanse the Face of my Spirit by Self-
examination.

To bathe in the waters of Life ; to wash off
    the Not-Human :
I come in Self-annihilation and the grandeur
    of Inspiration,
To cast off Rational Demonstration by Faith
    in the Saviour.

PROSE EXTRACTS.

AN ISLAND IN THE MOON.

From an unfinished MS.

(*Circa* 1789.)

CHAPTER I.

IN the Moon is a certain Island near by a mighty continent, which small island seems to have some affinity to England ; and what is more extraordinary, the people are so **much** alike, and their language so much the same, that you would think you were among your friends. In this island dwell three Philosophers, Suction, the Epicurean ; Quid, the Cynic ; and Lipsop, the Pythagorean. I call them by the names of those sects, though the sects are not ever mentioned there, as being quite out of date ; however, the things still remain, and the vanities are the same. The three Philosophers sat together thinking of nothing. In comes Etruscan Column, the Antiquarian, and, after an abundance of inquiries to no purpose, sat himself down and described something that nobody listened to.

So they were employed when Mrs. Gimblet came in ; the corners of her mouth seemed I

don't know how, but very odd, as if she hoped
you had not an ill opinion of her.   To be sure,
we are all poor creatures.   Well, she seated
herself, and seemed to listen with great atten-
tion while the Antiquarian seemed to be talking of virtuous cats ; but it was not so, she was
thinking of the shape of her eyes and mouth,
and he was thinking of his eternal fame.

The three Philosophers at this time were
each endeavouring to conceal his laughter,
not at them, but at his own imagination.
This was the situation of this improving company, when, in a great hurry, Inflammable
Gas, the Wind-finder, entered.   They seemed
to rise and salute each other.

Etruscan Column and Inflammable Gas fixed
their eyes on each other ; their tongues went
in question and answer, but their thoughts
were otherwise employed : " I don't like his
eyes," said Etruscan Column ; " He's a foolish
puppy," said Inflammable Gas, smiling on him.
The three Philosophers, the Cynic smiling,
the Epicurean seeming studying the flame of
the candle, and the Pythagorean playing with
the cat, listened with open mouths to the
edifying discourses.

" Sir," said the Antiquarian, " I have seen
these works, and I do affirm that they are no
such thing.   They seem to me to be the most
wretched, paltry, flimsy stuff that ever——"

"What d'ye say, what d'ye say?" said Inflammable Gas, "Why, why, I wish I could
see you write so." "Sir," said the Antiquarian, "according to my opinion, the author
is an errant blockhead." "Your reason, your
reason?" said Inflammable Gas, "Why, why,
I think it very abominable to call a man
a blockhead that you know nothing of."
"Reason, Sir," said the Antiquarian, "I'll
give you an example for your reason. As I
was walking along the street, I saw a vast
number **of** swallows on the rails of an old
Gothic square; they seemed to be going on
their passage, as Pliny says. As I was
looking up, a little *outré* fellow pulling me
by the sleeve cries, 'Pray, Sir, who **do all**
they belong to?' I turned myself about with
great contempt. Said I, 'Go along, you fool!'
'Fool,' said he, 'who do you call fool? I only
asked you a civil question.' I had a great
mind to have thrashed the fellow, only he was
bigger than I." Here Etruscan Column left
off. Inflammable Gas, recollecting himself,
"Indeed, I do not think the man was a fool,
for he seems to me to have been desirous of
inquiring into the works of nature." "Ha,
ha, ha," said the Pythagorean; it was re-
echoed by Inflammable Gas to overthrow the
argument. Etruscan Column then staring up
and clinching both his fists was prepared to

give a formal answer to the company. But
Obtuse Angle, entering the room, having made
a gentle bow, proceeded to empty his pockets
of a vast number of papers, turned about and
sat down, wiped his face with his pocket-
handkerchief, and, shutting his eyes, began
to scratch his head. "Well, gentlemen," said
he, "what is the cause of strife?" The Cynic
answered, "They are only quarrelling about
Voltaire." "Yes," said the Epicurean, "and
having a bit of fun with him." "And," said
the Pythagorean, "endeavouring to incor-
porate their souls with their bodies." Obtuse
Angle, giving a grin, said, "Voltaire understood nothing of the Mathematics, and a man
must be a fool, i'faith, not to understand the
Mathematics." Inflammable Gas, turning
round hastily in his chair, said, "Mathematics?
He found out a number of Queries in Philosophy." Obtuse Angle, shutting his eyes, and
saying that he always understood better when
he shut his eyes, "In the first place, it is no
use for a man to make Queries, but to solve
them : for a man may be a fool and make
Queries, but a man must have good sound
sense to solve them. A query and an answer
are as different as a straight line and a
crooked one. Secondly——" "I, I, I, aye,
secondly, Voltaire's a fool," says the Epicurean.
"Pooh," says the Mathematician, scratching

his head with double violence, " it is not worth
quarrelling about." The Antiquarian here
got up, and humming twice **to show the**
strength of his lungs, said, " But my Good
Sir, Voltaire was immersed **in matter, and**
seems to have understood very little **but** what
he saw before his eyes, like the Animal upon
the Pythagorean's lap, always playing with its
own **tail.**" " Ha, ha, **ha,**" said Inflammable
Gas, " He was the Glory of France. I have
got a bottle of air that would spread **a** Plague."
Here the Antiquarian shrugged his shoulders,
and was silent, while Inflammable Gas talked
for half an hour.

When Steelyard, the lawyer, coming in stalk-
ing, with an act of parliament in his hand,
said that it was a shameful thing that acts of
parliament should be in a free state ; it had
so engrossed his mind that he did not salute
the company.

Mrs. Gimblet drew her mouth downwards.

CHAPTER II.

Tilly Lally, the Tip-tippidist, Aradabo, the
dean of Morocco, Miss Gittipin, Mrs. Nanni-
cantipot, Mrs. Tigtagatist, Gibble Gabble, the
wife of Inflammable Gas, and Little Scopprell
entered the room.

If I have not presented you with every character in the piece call me ASS.

CHAPTER V.

Obtuse Angle, Scopprell, Aradabo, and Tilly Lally are all met in Obtuse Angle's study.

"Pray," said Aradabo, "is Chatterton a Mathematician?" "No;" said Obtuse Angle, "How can you be so foolish as to think he was?" "Oh, I did not think he was, I only asked," said Aradabo. "How can you think he was not, and ask if he was?" said Obtuse Angle. "Oh, no, Sir. I did think he was before you told me, but afterwards I thought he was not." Obtuse Angle said, "In the first place you thought he was, and then afterwards, when I said he was not, you thought he was not;—why, I know that!" "Oh, no, Sir, I thought he was not, but I asked to know whether he was." "How can that be?" said Obtuse Angle, "how could you ask, and think that he was not?" "Why," said he, "it came into my head that he was not." "Why, then," said Obtuse Angle, "you said that he was." "Did I say so? Law, I did not think I said that." "Did not he?" said Obtuse Angle. "Yes," said Scopprell. "But I meant," said

Aradabo, "—— I, I, I, can't think. Law, Sir, I wish you'd tell me how it is."

Then Obtuse Angle put his **chin in his** hand and said, "Whenever you think you **must** always think for yourself." "How, Sir," said Aradabo, "**whenever I** think **I must always** think for myself? I think I **do.** In the first place," said he, with a grin,——" "Poo, poo," said Obtuse Angle, "don't be a fool."

Then Tilly Lally took up a Quadrant and asked, "Is not this a sun-dial?" "Yes," said Scopprell, "but it's broke."

At this moment the three Philosophers entered, and lowering darkness hovered over the assembly.

"Come," said **the** Epicurean, "let's have some rum and water; and hang the Mathematics! Come, Aradabo, say something!" Then Aradabo began, "In the first place I think, I think in the first place that Chatterton was clever at Fissics, Follogy, Pistinology, Andology, Arography, Transmography, Phizography, Hogamy Hatomy, and hall that; but in the first place he eat wery little wickly, that is he slept very little, which he brought into a consumsion; and what was that that he took? Fissics, or somethink, and so died."

So all the people in the book entered into the room, and they could not talk any more to the present purpose.

A DESCRIPTIVE CATALOGUE OF PICTURES.

(1809.)

CHAUCER'S CANTERBURY PILGRIMS.

THE time chosen is early morning before sunrise, when the jolly company are just quitting the Tabarde Inn. The Knight and Squire, with the squire's yeomen, lead the procession ; next follow the youthful Abbess, her Nun, and three Priests. Her greyhounds attend her ;

> " Of small hounds had she that she fed
>   With roast flesh, milk, and wasted bread."

Next follow the Friar and Monk, then the Tapiser, the Pardoner, and the Sompnour and Manciple. After these " Our Host," who occupies the centre of the cavalcade, directs them to the Knight as the person who would be likely to commence their task of each telling a tale in their order. After the Host follow the Shipman, the Haberdasher, the Dyer, the Franklin, the Physician, the Plough-man, the Lawyer, the poor Parson, the Mer-chant, the Wife of Bath, the Miller, the Cook,

the Oxford Scholar, Chaucer himself ; and the
Reeve comes as Chaucer has described ;

" And ever he rode hinderest of the rout."

These last are issuing from the gateway **of**
the inn ; the Cook and the Wife of Bath are
both taking their morning's draught of comfort. Spectators stand at the gateway of the
inn, and are composed of an old man, a
woman, and children. The landscape is an
eastward view of the country from the Tabarde
Inn, in Southwark, as it may be supposed to
have appeared in Chaucer's time ; interspersed
with cottages and villages. The first beams
of the sun are seen above the horizon ; some
buildings and **spires** indicate the situation of
the Great **City.** **The** inn is **a** Gothic building,
which Thynne, in his glossary, says was **the**
lodging of the Abbot of Hyde, by Winchester.
On the inn is inscribed its title, and a proper
advantage is taken of this circumstance to
describe the subject of **the** picture. The
words written over the gateway of the inn
are as follows—" The Tabarde Inn, by Henry
Baillie, the lodgynge-house for Pilgrims who
journey to St. Thomas' Shrine at Canterbury."
The characters of Chaucer's Pilgrims are the
characters which compose all ages and nations
As one age falls another rises, different to
mortal sight, but to immortals only the same ;

for we see the same characters repeated again and again, in animals, vegetables, and minerals, and in men. Nothing new occurs in identical existence ; accident ever varies, substance can never suffer change or decay.

Of Chaucer's characters, as described in his "Canterbury Tales," some of the names or titles are altered by time, but the characters themselves for ever remain unaltered ; and, consequently, they are the physiognomies or lineaments of universal human life, beyond which nature never steps. Names alter, things never alter. I have known multitudes of those who would have been monks in the age of monkery, who in this deistical age are Deist. As Newton numbered the stars, and as Linnæus numbered the plants, so Chaucer numbered the classes of men. The Painter has consequently varied the heads and forms of his personages into all nature's varieties ; the horses he has also varied to accord to their riders ; the costume is correct according to authentic monuments.

The Knight and Squire, with the Squire's yeomen, lead the procession, as Chaucer has also placed them first in his prologue. The Knight is a true hero, a good, great, and wise man. His whole-length portrait on horse-back, as written by Chaucer, cannot be surpassed. He has spent his life in the

field, has ever been a conqueror, and is that
species of character which in every age stands
as the guardian of man against the oppressor.
His son is like him, with the germ **of** perhaps
greater perfection still, as he blends literature
and the arts with his warlike studies. Their
dress and their horses **are of** the first rate,
without ostentation, and with all the true
grandeur that unaffected simplicity, when in
high rank, always displays. The Squire's
Yeoman is also a great character, **a** man perfectly knowing in his profession :

> "And in his hand he bare a mighty bow."

Chaucer describes here a mighty man, one who
in war is the worthy attendant on noble heroes.

The Prioress follows these with her female
chaplain :

> "Another nonne **also** with her had she,
> That was her chaplain, and priestes three."

This lady is described also as of the first
rank, rich and honoured ; she has certain
peculiarities and little delicate affectations,
not unbecoming in her, being accompanied
with what is truly grand and really polite.
Her person and face Chaucer has described
with minuteness. It is very elegant, and was
the beauty of our ancestors till after Elizabeth's time, when voluptuousness and folly
began to be accounted beautiful. Her **com-**
panion and her three priests were no doubt

all perfectly delineated in those parts of
Chaucer's work which are now lost; we
ought to suppose them **suitable** attendants
on rank and fashion.

The Monk follows these with **the Friar.**
The painter has also grouped with these **the
Pardoner,** and the Sompnour, and the **Manciple,** and has here also introduced one of the
rich citizens of London—characters likely to
ride in company, all being **above the** common
rank in **life** or attendants **on those** who were
so.   For the Monk is described by Chaucer
as a man of the first rank in society, noble,
rich, and expensively attended; he is a leader
of the age, with certain humorous accompaniments in his character, that do not **de-
grade,** but render him an **object** of **dignified**
mirth, **but also with** other **accompaniments
not so** respectable.

The Friar **is a character also of a mixed
kind.**

> "A friar there was, a wanton and a merry."

But in his office he is said to be a "full
solemn man," eloquent, amorous, witty, and
satirical; young, handsome, and rich; he is
a complete rogue, with constitutional gaiety
enough to make him a master of all pleasures
of the world:

> "His neck was white as the flowerdelis,
>   Thereto strong he was as a champioun."

It is necessary here to speak of Chaucer's own character, that I may set certain mistaken critics right in their conception of the humour and fun that occur on the journey. Chaucer is himself the great poetical observer of men, who in every age is born to record and eternise its acts. This he does as a master, as a father and superior, who looks down on their little follies, from the Emperor to the Miller, sometimes with severity, oftener with joke and sport. Accordingly Chaucer has made his Monk a great tragedian, one who studied poetical art. So much so, that the generous Knight is, in the compassionate dictates of his soul, compelled to cry out :

> "'Ho,' quoth the Knight, 'good sir, no more of this,
> That ye have said is right ynough, I wis,
> And mokell more ; for little heaviness
> Is right enough for much folk, as I guess.
> I say, for me, it is a great disease,
> Whereas men have been in wealth and ease,
> To heare of their sudden fall, alas !
> And the contrary is joy and solas.'"

The Monk's definition of tragedy in the proem to his tale is worth repeating :

> " Tragedy is to tell a certain story,
> As olde books us maken memory,
> Of him that stood in great prosperity,
> And be fallen out of high degree
> Into misery and ended wretchedly !"

O

Though a man of luxury, pride, and pleasure, he is a master of art and learning, though affecting to despise it. Those who think that to the proud Huntsman and noble House-keeper Chaucer's Monk is intended for a buffoon or burlesque character, know little of Chaucer. For the Host who follows this group and holds the centre of the cavalcade is a first-rate character, and his jokes are no trifles ; they are always, though uttered with audacity, equally free with the Lord and Peasant ; they are always substantially and weightily expressive of knowledge and expe-rience. Henry Baillie, the keeper of the greatest inn of the greatest city—for such was the Tabarde Inn in Southwark, near London—our Host, was also a leader of the age.

By way of illustration, I instance Shake-speare's witches in "Macbeth." Those who dress them for the stage consider them as wretched old women, and not as Shake-peare intended, the Goddesses of Destiny. This shows how much Chaucer has been misunderstood in *his* sublime work. Shake-speare's fairies also are the rulers of the vegetable world, and so are Chaucer's. Let them be so considered, and then the poet will be understood, and not else.

But I have omitted to speak of a very

prominent character, the Pardoner, the Age's
Knave, who always commands and domineers
over the high and low vulgar. This man is
sent in every age for a rod and scourge, and
for a blight, for a trial of men, to divide the
classes of men; he is in the most holy sanc-
tuary, and he is suffered by Providence for
wise ends, and has also his use, and grand
leading destiny.

His companion, the Sompnour, is also a
devil of the first magnitude, grand, terrific,
rich, and honoured in the rank of which he
holds the destiny. The uses to society are
perhaps equal of the Devil and of the Angel;
their sublimity who can dispute?

> " In daunger had he at his owne gise,
>   The younge girles of his diocese,
>   And he knew well their counsel," &c.

The principal figure in the next group is the
Good Parson: an Apostle, a real Messenger
of Heaven, sent in every age for its light and
its warmth. This man is beloved and vene-
rated by all, and neglected by all: he serves
all, and is served by none. He is, according
to Christ's definition, the greatest of his age;
yet he is a Poor Parson of a town. Read
Chaucer's description of the Good Parson,
and bow the head and knee to Him who, in
every age, sends us such a burning and a

shining light.   Search, O ye rich and powerful,
for these men, and obey their counsel ; then
shall the Golden Age return.   But alas ! you
will not easily distinguish him from the Friar
or the Pardoner ; they also are "full solemn
men," and their counsel you will continue to
follow.

I have placed by his side the Sergeant-at-
Lawe, who appears delighted to ride in his
company, and between him and his brother
the Ploughman, as I wish men of law would
always ride with them and take their counsel,
especially in all difficult points.   Chaucer's
Lawyer is a character of great venerable-
ness, a Judge, and a real master of the juris-
prudence of his age.

The Doctor of Physic is in this group, and
the Franklin, the voluptuous country gentle-
man ; contrasted with the Physician, and, on
his other hand, with two Citizens of London.

Chaucer's characters live age after age.
Every age is a Canterbury Pilgrimage ; we
all pass on, each sustaining one or other of
these characters ; nor can a child be born who
is not one of these characters of Chaucer.
The Doctor of Physic is described as the first
of his profession : perfect, learned, completely
Master and Doctor in his art.   Thus the
reader will observe that Chaucer makes every
one of his characters perfect in his kind ;

every one is an Antique Statue, the image **of a** class, and not an imperfect individual.

This group also would furnish substantial matter, on which volumes might **be** written. The Franklin is one who keeps open table, who is the genius of eating and drinking, the Bacchus; as the Doctor of Physic is the Æsculapius, the Host is the Silenus, the Squire is the Apollo, the Miller is Hercules, &c. Chaucer's characters are a description of the eternal Principles that exist in all ages. The Franklin is voluptuousness itself most **nobly** portrayed :

> " It snowed in his house of meat and drink."

The Ploughman **is** simplicity itself, with **wis**dom and strength for its stamina. Chaucer has divided the ancient character of Hercules between his Miller and his Ploughman. Benevolence is the Ploughman's great charac**teristic ; he is** thin with excessive labour, and **not with old** age as some have supposed :

> " He woulde thresh and thereto dike and delve,
> For Christe's sake, for every poore wight,
> Withouten hire, if it lay in his might."

Visions of these eternal principles or characters of human life appear to poets in all ages : the Grecian gods were the ancient

Cherubim of Phœnicia ; but the Greeks, and since them the Moderns, have neglected to subdue the gods of Priam. These gods are visions of the eternal attributes, or divine names, which, when erected into gods, become destructive to humanity. They ought to be the servants, and not the masters, of man or of society. They ought to be made to sacrifice to Man, and not man compelled to sacrifice to them ; for, when separated from man or humanity, who is Jesus the Saviour, the vine of eternity ? They are thieves and rebels, they are destroyers.

The Ploughman of Chaucer is Hercules in his supreme eternal state, divested of his spectrous shadow, which is the Miller, a terrible fellow, such as exists in all times and places, for the trial of men, to astonish every neighbourhood with brutal strength and courage, to get rich and powerful, to curb the pride of man.

The Reeve and the Manciple are two characters of the most consummate worldly wisdom. The Shipman or Sailor is a similar genius of Ulyssean art, but with the highest courage superadded.

The Citizens and their Cook are each leaders of a class. Chaucer has been somehow made to number four citizens, which would make his whole company, himself included, thirty-one.

But he says there were but nine-and-twenty **in** his company :

"Full nine-and-twenty in **a** company."

The Webbe, or Weaver, and the Tapiser, **or** Tapestry Weaver, appear to me to be **the** same person ; but this is only an opinion, for full nine-and-twenty may signify one more or less. But I dare say Chaucer wrote "A Webbe Dyer," that is, a Cloth Dyer ;

"A Webbe Dyer and a Tapiser."

The merchant cannot **be** one of the Three Citizens, as his dress is different, and his character is more marked, whereas, Chaucer says of his rich citizens :

"All were yclothed in o liverie."

The character of Women Chaucer has divided into two classes, the Lady Prioress **and** the Wife of Bath. Are not these leaders of the ages of men ? The Lady Prioress in some ages predominates, and in some the Wife of Bath, in whose character Chaucer has been equally minute and **exact,** because she is also a scourge and a blight. I shall say no more of her, nor expose what Chaucer **has** left hidden ; let the young reader study **what** he has said of her—it is useful as a scarecrow. There are of such characters born too many for the peace of the world.

I come at length to the Clerk of Oxenford. This character varies from that of Chaucer, as the contemplative philosopher varies from the poetical genius. There are always these two classes of learned sages, the poetical and the philosophical. The painter has put them side by side, as if the youthful clerk had put himself under the tuition of the mature poet. Let the philosopher always be the servant and scholar of inspiration, and all will be happy.

Such are the characters that compose this picture, which was painted in self-defence against the insolent and envious imputation of unfitness for finished and scientific art ; and this imputation most artfully and industriously endeavoured to be propagated among the public by ignorant hirelings. The Painter courts comparison with his competitors, who having received fourteen hundred guineas, and more, from the profits of *his* designs in that well-known work, Designs for Blair's "Grave," have left him to shift for himself ; while others more obedient to an employer's opinions and directions are employed, at a great expense, to produce works in succession to his by which they acquired public patronage. This has hitherto been

his lot—to get patronage for others and then
to be left and neglected, and his work, which
gained that patronage, cried down as eccen-
tricity and madness—as unfinished and neglected by the artist's violent temper; he is
sure the works now exhibited will give the
lie to such aspersions.

Those who say that men are led by interest
are knaves. A knavish character will often
say, Of what interest is it to me to do so and
so? I answer, Of none at all, but the contrary, as you know well. It is of malice and
envy that you have done this; hence I am
aware of you, because I know that you act
not from interest, but from malice, even to
your own destruction. It is therefore become
a duty which Mr. B. owes to the public, who
have alway recognised him and patronised
him, however hidden by artifices, that he
should not suffer such things to be done, or
be hindered from the public exhibition of his
finished productions by any calumnies in
future.

The character and expression in this picture could never have been produced with
Rubens' light and shadow, or with Rembrandt's, or anything Venetian or Flemish.
The Venetian and Flemish practice is broken
lines, broken masses, and broken colours:
Mr. B.'s practice is unbroken lines, unbroken

masses, and unbroken colours. Their art is to lose form; his art is to find form and to keep it. His arts are opposite to theirs in all things.

As there is a class of men whose whole delight is in the destruction of men, so there is a class of artists whose whole art and science is fabricated for this purpose of destroying Art. Who these are is soon known: "by their works ye shall know them." All who endeavour to raise up a style against Raphael, Michael Angelo, and the Antique; those who separate Painting from Drawing; who look if a picture is well drawn, and, if it is, immediately cry out that it cannot be well coloured—those are the men. But to show the stupidity of this class of men, nothing need be done but to examine my rival's prospectus.

The two first characters in Chaucer, the Knight and the Squire, he has put amongst his rabble; and indeed his prospectus calls the Squire "the fop of Chaucer's age." Now hear Chaucer;

> "Of his stature, he was even length,
> And wonderly deliver, and of great strength;
> And he had be sometime in Chivauchy,
> In Flanders, in Artois, and in Picardy,
> And borne him well as of so litele space."

Was this a fop?

> "Well could he sit a horse, and faire ride.
> He could songs make, and eke well indite,
> Joust, and eke dance, portray, and well write."

Was this a fop?

> "Curteis he was, and meek, and serviceable;
> And kerft before his fader at the table."

Was *this* a fop?

It is the same with all his characters; he has done all by chance, or perhap his fortune, money, money. According to his prospectus he has Three Monks; these he cannot find in Chaucer, who has only One Monk, and that no vulgar character as he has endeavoured to make him. When men cannot read, they should not pretend to paint. To be sure Chaucer is a little difficult to him who has only blundered over novels or catchpenny trifles of booksellers; yet a little pains ought to be taken, even by the ignorant and weak. He has put the Reeve, a vulgar fellow, between his Knight and Squire, as if he was resolved to go contrary in everything to Chaucer, who says of the Reeve:

> "And ever he rode hinderest of the rout."

In this manner he has jumbled his dumb dollies together, and is praised by his equals for it; for both himself and his friend are equally masters of Chaucer's language. They both think the Wife of Bath is a young, beautiful, blooming damsel ; and H. says that she is the "Fair Wife of Bath," and that "the Spring appears in her cheeks." Now hear what Chaucer has made her say of herself, who is no modest one :

> " But Lord ! when it remembreth me
>   Upon my youth, and on my jollity,
>   It tickleth me about the hearte root.
>   Unto this day it doth my hearte boot
>   That I have had my world as in my time ;
>   But age, alas ! that all will envenime,
>   Hath me bereft, my beauty and my pith
>   Let go ; farewell ! the devil go therewith !
>   The flour is gone, there is no more to tell :
>   The bran, as best I can, I now mote sell ;
>   And yet to be right merry, will I fond
>   Now forth to telle of my fourth husband."

She has had four husbands, a fit subject for this Painter ; yet the painter ought to be very much offended with his friend H., who has called his "a common scene," and "very ordinary forms," which is the truest part of all ; for it is so, and very wretchedly so, indeed. What merit can there be in a picture of which such words are spoken with truth ?

But the prospectus says that the Painter has represented Chaucer himself as a knave

who thrusts himself among honest people
to make game of and laugh at them ;
though I must do justice to the Painter, and
say that he has made him look more like a
fool than a knave. But it appears in all the
writings of Chaucer, and particularly in his
" Canterbury Tales," that he was very devout,
and paid respect to true enthusiastic supersti-
tion. He has laughed at his knave and fools,
as I do now. But he has respected his True
Pilgrims, who are a majority of his company,
and not thrown together in the random
manner that Mr. S. has done. Chaucer has
nowhere called the Ploughman old, worn out
with " age and labour," as the prospectus has
represented him, and says that the picture has
done so too. He is worn down with labour,
but not with age. How spots of brown and
yellow, smeared about at random, can be
either young or old, I cannot see. It may be
an old man ; it may be a young one : it may
be anything that a prospectus pleases. But
I know that where there are no lineaments,
there can be no character. And what con-
noisseurs call touch, I know by experience,
must be the destruction of all character and
expression, as it is of every lineament.

The scene of Mr. S.'s picture is by Dulwich
Hills, which was not the way to Canterbury ;
but perhaps the Painter thought he would

give them a ride round about, because they
were a burlesque set of scarecrows not worth
any man's respect or care.

But the Painter's thoughts being always
upon gold, he has introduced a character
that Chaucer has not—namely, a Goldsmith,
for so the prospectus tells us. Why he has
introduced a Goldsmith, and what is the wit
of it, the prospectus does not explain. But
it takes care to mention the reserve and
modesty of the Painter ; this makes a good
epigram enough :

> " The fox, the mole, the beetle, and the bat,
>   By sweet reserve and modesty get fat."

But the prospectus tells us that the Painter
has introduced a " Sea Captain." Chaucer
has a Shipman, a Sailor, a Trading Master of
a Vessel, called by courtesy Captain, as every
master of a boat is ; but this does not make
him a Sea Captain. Chaucer has purposely
omitted such a personage, as it only exists in
certain periods : it is the soldier by sea. He
who would be a soldier in inland nations, is a
sea-captain in commercial nations.

All is misconceived, and its mis-execution
is equal to its misconception. I have no
objection to Rubens and Rembrandt being
employed, or even to their living in a palace;
but it shall not be at the expense of Raphael

or Michael Angelo living in a cottage and
in contempt and derision.   I have been
scorned long enough by these fellows, who
owe to me all that they have ; it shall **be so**
no longer :

" I found them blind, I taught them how to see ;
   And now they know neither themselves nor me."

THE ANCIENT BRITONS.

*In the last Battle of King Arthur, only
three Britons escaped—these were, the Strongest Man, the Beautifullest Man, and the
Ugliest Man.   These three marched through
the field unsubdued, as gods, and the sun of
Britain set, but shall arise again with tenfold
splendour when Arthur shall awake from
sleep, and resume his dominion over earth
and ocean.*

The three general classes of men who are
represented by the most Beautiful, the most
Strong, **and** the most Ugly, could not be
represented by any historical facts but those
of our own country, the ancient Britons, without violating costume.   The Britons (say
historians) were naked civilised men, learned,
studious, abstruse in thought and contemplation ; naked, simple, plain in their acts and
manners ; wiser than after ages.   They were

overwhelmed by brutal arms; all but a small
remnant, Strength, Beauty, and Ugliness,
escaped the wreck, and remained for ever
unsubdued, age after age.

The British Antiquities are now in the
artist's hands; all his visionary contempla-
tions relating to his own country and its
ancient glory, when it was, as it again shall
be, the source of learning and inspiration
(Arthur was a name for the Constellation
Arcturus, or Bootes, the Keeper of the North
Pole); and all the fables of Arthur and his
Round Table; of the warlike naked Britons of
Merlin; of Arthur's conquest of the whole
world; of his death or sleep, and promise to
return again; of the Druid monuments or
temples; of the pavement of Watling Street;
of London Stone; of the caverns in Cornwall,
Wales, Derbyshire, and Scotland; of the
Giants of Ireland and Britain; of the ele-
mental beings, called by us by the general
name of Fairies; and of these three who
escaped, namely, Beauty, Strength, and Ugliness. Mr. B. has on his hand poems of the
highest antiquity. Adam was a Druid, and
Noah; also Abraham was called to succeed
the Druidical age, which began to turn allegoric and mental signification into corporeal
command, whereby human sacrifice would
have depopulated the earth. All these things

are written in Eden. The Artist is an inhabi-
tant of that happy country, and if everything
goes on as it has begun, the world of vegetation and generation may expect to be opened
again to heaven, through Eden, as it was **in**
the beginning.

The Strong Man represents the human sublime; the Beautiful Man represents the human
pathetic, which was in the wars of Eden
divided into male and female; the Ugly Man
represents the human reason. They were
originally one man, who was fourfold; he was
self-divided, and his real humanity slain on
the stems of generation, and the form of the
fourth was like the Son of God. How he
became divided is a subject of great sublimity
and pathos. The artist has written **it** under
inspiration, and will, if God please, publish
it; it is voluminous, and contains the ancient
history of Britain, and the world of Satan
and of Adam.

In the meantime he has painted this
picture, which supposes that in the reign
of that British Prince, who lived in the fifth
century, they were remains of those naked
Heroes in the Welsh mountains; they are
there now—Gray saw them in the person of
his Bard on Snowdon; there they dwell in
naked simplicity; happy is he who can see
and converse with them above the shadows

P

of generation and death.   The Giant Albion
was Patriarch of the Atlantic; his is the
Atlas of the Greeks, one of those the Greeks
call Titans.   The Stories of Arthur are the
acts of Albion applied to a Prince of the fifth
century, who conquered Europe, and held
the empire of the world in the dark age,
which the Romans never again recovered.
In this picture, believing with Milton the
ancient British History, Mr. B. has done
all as the ancients did, and as all the
moderns who are worthy of fame—given the
historical fact in its poetical vigour, so as it
always happens, and not in that dull way
that some historians pretend, who being
weakly organised themselves cannot see
either miracle or prodigy : all is to them a
dull round of probabilities and possibilities ;
but the history of all times and places is
nothing else but improbabilities and impossi-
bilities—what we should say was impossible
if we did not see it always before our eyes.

The antiquities of every nation under heaven
are no less sacred than those of the Jews.
They are the same thing ; as Jacob Bryant
and all antiquaries have proved.   How other
antiquities came to be neglected and dis-
believed, while those of the Jews are collected
and arranged, is an inquiry worthy of both
the Antiquarian and the Divine.   All had

originally one language and one religion;
this was the religion of Jesus, the everlasting
Gospel. Antiquity preaches the Gospel of
Jesus. The reasoning historian, turner and
twister of causes and consequences—such as
Hume, Gibbon, and Voltaire—cannot with all
his artifice turn or twist one fact, or disarrange
self-evident action and reality. Reasons and
opinions concerning acts are not history;
acts themselves alone are history, and these
are not the exclusive property **of** either
Hume, Gibbon, or Voltaire, Echard, Rapin,
Plutarch, or Herodotus. Tell me the acts,
O historian, and leave me to reason upon
them as I please; away with your reasoning
and your rubbish! All that is not action is
not worth reading. Tell me the What; I
do not want you to tell me the Why, and
the How; I can find that out myself as well
as you can, and I will not be fooled by you
into opinions that you please to impose, to
disbelieve what you think improbable or
impossible. His opinion who does not
see spiritual agency is not worth any man's
reading; he who rejects a fact because it is
improbable must reject all history, and retain
doubts only.

It has been said to the artist, take the
Apollo for the model of your Beautiful Man,
and the Hercules for your Strong Man, and

the Dancing Faun for your Ugly Man. Now
he comes to his trial. He knows what he
does is not inferior to the grandest Antiques.
Superior it cannot be, for human power
cannot go beyond either what he does or
what they have done; it is the gift of God,
it is inspiration and vision. He had resolved
to emulate these precious remains of antiquity; he has done so, and the result you
behold : his ideas of strength and beauty have
not been greatly different. Poetry as it
exists now on earth in the various remains of
ancient authors, Music as it exists in old
tunes or melodies, Painting and Sculpture as
they exist in the remains of antiquity and in
the works of more modern genius—each is
Inspiration and cannot be surpassed : it is
perfect and eternal. Milton, Shakespeare,
Michael Angelo, Raphael, the finest specimens of Ancient Sculpture, and Painting, and
Architecture, Gothic, Grecian, Hindoo, and
Egyptian, are the extent of the human mind.
The human mind cannot go beyond the gift
of God, the Holy Ghost. To suppose that
Art can go beyond the finest specimens of Art
that are now in the world is not knowing what
Art is; it is being blind to the gifts of the Spirit.

It will be necessary for the Painter to say
something concerning his ideas of Beauty,
Strength, and Ugliness.

The Beauty that is annexed and appended
to folly, **is** a lamentable accident and error
of the mortal and perishing life ; **it** does but
seldom happen, but with this unnatural **mix-
ture** the sublime **Artist** can have nothing **to**
do ; it is fit for **the** burlesque. The Beauty
proper for sublime art is lineaments, or forms
and features that are capable of being the
receptacles of intellect; accordingly the Painter
has given in his Beautiful Man his own ideas
of intellectual Beauty. The **face and** limbs
that deviate or alter least, from infancy to old
age, are the face and limbs of greatest beauty
and perfection.

The Ugly, likewise, **when** accompanied
and annexed **to** imbecility and disease, **is a**
subject **for burlesque,** and not for historical
grandeur. The Artist has imagined his Ugly
Man one approaching to the beast in features
and form, his forehead small, without frontals,
his jaws large, his nose high on the ridge,
and narrow his chest, and the stamina of
his make comparatively little, and his joints
and his extremities large, his eyes with scarce
any whites, narrow and cunning, and everything tending toward what is truly Ugly—
the incapability of intellect.

The Artist has considered his Strong Man
as a receptacle of Wisdom, a sublime energiser; his features and limbs do not spindle out

into length without strength, nor are they too large and unwieldy for his brain and bosom. Strength consists in accumulation of power to the principal seat, and from thence a regular graduation and subordination ; strength is compactness, not extent nor bulk.

The Strong Man acts from conscious superiority, and marches on in fearless dependence on the divine decrees raging with the inspirations of a prophetic mind. The Beautiful Man acts from duty and anxious solicitude for the fates of those for whom he combats. The Ugly Man acts from love of carnage, and delights in the savage barbarities of war, rushing with sportive precipitation into the very teeth of the affrighted enemy.

The Roman Soldiers, rolled together in a heap before them, "like the rolling thing before the whirlwind," show each a different character and a different expression of fear, or revenge, or envy, or blank horror, or amazement, or devout wonder and unresisting awe. The dead and the dying, Britons naked mingled with armed Romans, strew the field beneath. Among these the last of the Bards who was capable of attending warlike deeds is seen falling, outstretched among the dead and the dying, singing to his harp in the pains of death.

Distant among the mountains are Druid
Temples similar to Stonehenge.   The Sun
sets behind the mountains, **bloody** with the
day of battle.

The flush of health in flesh exposed to **the**
open air, nourished by the spirits of **forests**
and floods, **in that** ancient happy period
which history has recorded, cannot be the
sickly daubs of Titian or Rubens.   Where
will the copier of nature, as **it** now is, find a
civilised man who has been accustomed to
go naked ?   Imagination only can furnish us
with colouring appropriate, such as is found
in the Frescoes of Raphael and Michael
Angelo ;   the disposition of forms   always
directs colouring in works of true **art**.   As to
a modern man, stripped from his load **of**
clothing, he **is** like a dead corpse.   **Hence**
Rubens, Titian, Correggio, and all of that
class, are like leather and chalk ; their men
are like leather and their women like chalk ;
for the disposition of their forms will not
admit **of** grand colouring.   In Mr. B.'s
Britons the blood is seen to circulate in their
limbs ; he defies competition in colouring.

SIBYLLINE LEAVES.

ON HOMER'S POETRY.

EVERY poem must necessarily be a perfect unity, but why Homer's is peculiarly so I cannot tell: he has told the story of Bellerophon, and omitted the Judgment of Paris, which is not only a part but a principal part of Homer's subject. But when a work has unity, it is as much so in a part as in the whole. The torso is as much a unity as the Laocöon. As unity is the cloak of folly, so goodness is the cloak of knavery. Those who will have unity exclusively in Homer come out with a moral like a sting in the tail. Aristotle says characters are either good or bad; now, goodness or badness has nothing to do with character. An apple-tree, a pear-tree, a horse, a lion, are characters; but a good apple-tree or a bad is an apple-tree still. A horse is not more a lion for being a bad horse—that is its character: its goodness or badness is another consideration.

It is the same with the moral of a whole poem as with the moral goodness of its parts. Unity and morality are secondary considera-

tions, and belong to Philosophy, and not to
Poetry—to exception, and not to rule—to
accident, and not to substance. The ancients
called it eating of the Tree of Good and Evil.

The Classics **it** is, the Classics, **and not**
Goths or monks, that desolate Europe with
wars.

A VISION OF THE LAST JUDGMENT.

THE Last Judgment is not fable, or allegory, but vision.   Fable, or allegory, is a totally distinct and inferior kind of poetry. Vision, or imagination, is a representation of what actually exists, really and unchangeably. Fable, or allegory, is formed by the daughters of Memory.   Imagination is surrounded by the daughters of Inspiration, who, in the aggregate, are called Jerusalem.   Fable is allegory, but what critics call *the fable* is vision itself.   The Hebrew Bible and the Gospel of Jesus are not allegory, but eternal vision, or imagination of all that exists.   Note here that fable, or allegory, is seldom without some vision.   "Pilgrim's Progress" is full of it ; the Greek poets the same.   But allegory and vision ought to be known as two distinct things, and so called for the sake of eternal life.   The ancients produce fable when they assert that Jupiter usurped the throne of his father, Saturn, and brought on an iron age, and begot on Mnemosyne, or memory, the great Muses, which are not inspiration, as the Bible is.   Reality was forgot, and the varieties of time and space only remembered, and called

reality. The Greeks represented Chronos,
or Time, as a very aged man. This is fable,
but the real vision of Time is an eternal
youth. I have, however, somewhat accom-
modated my figure of Time to the common
opinion; as I myself am also infected with
it, and my vision is also infected, and I see
Time aged—alas! too much so. Allegories
are things that relate to moral virtues. Moral
virtues do not exist: they are allegories and
dissimulations. But Time and Space are
real beings, a male and a female; Time is a
man, Space is a woman, and her masculine
portion is Death. Such is the mighty difference between allegoric fables and spiritual
mystery. Let it here be noted that the Greek
fables originated in spiritual mystery and real
vision, which are lost and clouded in fable
and allegory; while the Hebrew Bible and
the Greek Gospel are genuine, preserved by
the Saviour's mercy. The nature of my work
is visionary, or imaginative; it is an endeavour
to restore what the ancients called the Golden
Age.

Plato has made Socrates say that poets
and prophets do not know or understand
what they write or utter. This is a most
pernicious falsehood. If they do not, pray,
is an inferior kind to be called "knowing"?
Plato confutes himself.

The Last Judgment is one of these stupendous visions. I have represented it as I saw it. To different people it appears differently, as everything else does.

In eternity one thing never changes into another thing; each identity is eternal. Consequently, Apuleius' Golden Ass, and Ovid's Metamorphoses, and others of the like kind are fable; yet they contain vision in a sublime degree, being derived from real vision in more ancient writings. Lot's wife being changed into a pillar of salt alludes to the mortal body being rendered a permanent statue, but not changed or transformed into another identity, while it retains its own individuality. A man can never become ass nor horse; some are born with shapes of men who are both; but eternal identity is one thing, and corporeal vegetation is another thing. Changing water into wine by Jesus, and into blood by Moses, relates to vegetable nature also.

The nature of visionary fancy, or imagination, is very little known; and the eternal nature and permanence of its ever-existent images are considered as less permanent than the things of vegetable and generative nature. Yet the oak dies as well as the lettuce; but its eternal image or individuality never dies, but renews by its seed. Just so, the imagina-

tive image returns by the seed of contemplative thought. The writings of **the** prophets
illustrate these conceptions of the visionary
fancy by their various sublime **and** divine
images as seen in the worlds of vision.

The world **of** imagination is the world **of**
eternity. It is the divine bosom into which
we shall all go after the death **of the** vegetated
body. This world of imagination is infinite
and eternal, whereas the world of generation,
or vegetation, is finite and temporal. There
exist in that **eternal** world the realities of
everything which we see **reflected** in this
vegetable glass of nature.

All things are comprehended **in these**
eternal forms **in** the divine **body of the**
Saviour, the true vine of eternity, **who** appeared to me as coming to judgment among
His saints, and throwing off the temporal,
that the eternal might be established. Around
Him were seen the images of existence accord-
ing to a certain order, suited to my imagina-
tive eye, as follows :

Jesus seated between **the** two pillars,
Jachin **and** Boaz, with the word divine of
revelation **on** His Knee, and on each side
the four-and-twenty elders sitting in judgment : the heavens opening around Him by
unfolding the clouds around His throne.
The old heavens and the old earth are passing

away, and the new heavens and the new
earth descending : a sea of fire issues from
before the throne. Adam and Eve appear
first before the judgment-seat, in humiliation ;
Abel surrounded by innocents ; and Cain,
with the flint in his hand with which he slew
his brother, falling with the head downwards.
From the cloud on which Eve stands Satan
is seen falling headlong, wound round by the
tail of the serpent, whose bulk, nailed to the
cross round which he wreathes, is falling into
the abyss. Sin is also represented as a
female bound in one of the serpent's folds,
surrounded by her fiends. Death is chained
to the cross, and Time falls together with
Death, dragged down by a demon crowned
with laurel. Another demon, with a key,
has the charge of Sin, and is dragging her
down by the hair. Beside them a figure is
seen, scaled with iron scales from head to
feet, precipitating himself into the sword and
balances ; he is Og the King of Bashan.

On the right, beneath the cloud on which
Abel kneels, is Abraham, with Sarah and
Isaac, also with Hagar and Ishmael on the
left. Abel kneels on a bloody cloud, descriptive of those churches before the Flood,
that they were filled with blood and fire and
vapour of smoke. Even till Abraham's time
the vapour and heat were not extinguished.

These states exist now. Man passes on, but
states remain for ever ; he passes through
them like a traveller, who may as well suppose
that the places he has passed through exist
no more, as **a man** may suppose **that the**
states **he has passed** through exist no **more :**
everything is eternal.

Beneath Ishmael is Mahomed ; and beneath the falling figure of Cain is Moses,
casting his tables of stone into the deeps. It
ought to **be** understood that the persons
Moses and Abraham are **not** here meant, but
the states signified by those names ; the individuals being representations, or visions, of
those states, as they were revealed to mortal
man in the series of divine revelations, as they
are written in the Bible. These various states
I have seen in my imagination. When distant, they appear as one man ; but as you
approach they appear multitudes of nations.

Abraham hovers above his posterity, which
appear as multitudes of children ascending
from **the** earth, surrounded by stars, as it was
said, "As the stars of heaven for multitude."
Jacob and his twelve sons hover beneath the
feet of Abraham, and receive their children
from the earth. I have seen, when at a distance, multitudes of men in harmony appear
like a single infant, sometimes in the arms of
a female. This represented the Church.

But to proceed with the description of those on the left hand. Beneath the cloud on which Moses kneels are two figures, a male and a female, chained together by the feet. They represent those who perished by **the** Flood. Beneath them a multitude of their associates are seen falling headlong. By the side of them is a mighty fiend with a book in his hand, which is shut : he represents the person named in Isaiah, c. xxii. v. 20, Eliakim, the son of Hilkiah. He drags Satan down headlong. He is crowned with oak. By the side of the scaled figure, representing Og, King of Bashan, is a figure with a basket, emptying out the varieties of riches and worldly honours. He is Araunah, the Jebusite, master of the threshing-floor. Above him are two figures elevated on a cloud, representing the Pharisees, who plead their own righteousness before the throne ; they are weighed down by two fiends. Beneath the man with the basket are three fiery fiends, with grey beards and scourges of fire : they represent cruel laws. They scourge a group of figures down into the deeps. Beneath them are various figures in attitudes of contention, representing various states of misery, which, alas ! every one on earth is liable to enter into, and against which we should all watch. The ladies will be pleased to see that I have represented the Furies by three men, and not by three women. It is not because I think the ancients wrong ; but they will be pleased to remember that mine is vision, and not fable. The spectator may suppose them clergymen in the pulpit, scourging sin, instead of forgiving it.

The earth beneath these falling groups of figures is rocky and burning, and seems as if convulsed by earthquakes. A great city, on fire, is seen in the distance. The armies are fleeing upon the mountains. On the foreground Hell is opened, and many figures are descending into it down stone steps, and beside a gate beneath a rock, where Sin and Death are to be closed eternally by that fiend who carries the key in one hand, and drags them down with the other. On the rock, and above the gate, a fiend with wings urges the wicked onward with fiery darts. He is Hazael, the Syrian, who drives abroad all those who rebel against their Saviour. Beneath the steps is Babylon, represented by a king crowned, grasping his sword and his sceptre. He is just awakened out of his grave. Around him are other kingdoms arising to judgment, represented in this picture by single personages, according to the description in the Prophets. The figure dragging up a woman by her hair represents the In-

quisition, as do those contending in the sides
of the pit; and, in particular, the man strang-
ling a woman represents a cruel church.

Two persons, one in purple, the other in
scarlet, are descending down the steps into
the pit.   These are Caiaphas and Pilate; two
states where all those reside who calumniate
and murder under pretence to holiness and
justice.   Caiaphas has a blue flame like a
mitre on his head; Pilate has bloody hands,
that can never be cleansed.   The females
behind them represent the females belonging
to such states, who are under perpetual terrors
and vain dreams, plots, and secret deceit.
Those figures that descend into the flames
before Caiaphas and Pilate are Judas and
those of his class.   Achitophel is also here,
with the cord in his hand.

Between the figures of Adam and Eve
appears a fiery gulf descending from the sea
of fire before the throne.   In this cataract
four angels descend headlong with four
trumpets to awake the dead.   Beneath these
is the seat of the harlot, named Mystery in
the Revelation.   She is seized by two beings,
each with three heads: they represent vegetative existence.   As it is written in the
Revelation, they strip her naked, and burn
her with fire.   It represents the eternal con-
sumption of vegetable life and death, with its

lusts. **The** wreathed torches in their hands represent eternal fire, which is the fire of generation or vegetation; it is **an** eternal consummation. Those who are blessed with imaginative **vision see** this eternal female, and tremble **at** what others fear not : while they **despise** and laugh at what others fear. Beneath her feet is a flaming cavern, in which **are** seen her kings, and councillors, and warriors, descending into flames, lamenting, and looking upon her in astonishment and terror, and Hell is opened beneath her seat; on the left hand, the great Red Dragon, with seven heads and ten horns. He has a book of accusations, lying on the rock, open before him. He is bound in chains by two strong demons : they are Gog and Magog, who have been compelled to subdue their master (Ezekiel, c. xxxviii. v. 8) with their hammer and tongs, about to new-create the seven-headed kingdoms. The graves beneath are opened, and the dead awake, and obey the call of the trumpet : those on the right hand awake in joy, those on the left in horror. Beneath the Dragon's cavern a skeleton begins to animate, starting into life at the trumpet's sound, while the wicked contend with each other on the brink of perdition. On the right, a youthful couple are awaked by their children ; an aged patriarch is awaked by his aged wife :

he is Albion, our ancestor, patriarch of the
Atlantic Continent, whose history preceded
that of the Hebrews, and in whose sleep, or
chaos, creation began. The good woman is
Britannica, the wife of Albion. Jerusalem is
their daughter. Little infants creep out of the
flowery mould into the green fields of the
blessed, who, in various joyful companies,
embrace and ascend to meet eternity.

The persons who ascend to meet the Lord
in the clouds with power and great glory, are
representations of those states described in
the Bible under the names of the Fathers
before and after the Flood. Noah is seen in
the midst of these, canopied by a rainbow.
On his right hand Shem, and on his left
Japhet. These three persons represent Poetry,
Painting, and Music, the three powers in man
of conversing with Paradise, which the Flood
did not sweep away. Above Noah is the
Church Universal, represented by a woman
surrounded by infants. There is such a state
in eternity : it is composed of the innocent
civilised heathen and the uncivilised savage,
who, having not the law, do by nature the
things contained in the law. This state
appears like a female crowned with stars,
driven into the wilderness : she has the moon
under her feet. The aged figure with wings,
having a writing tablet, and taking account of

the numbers who arise, is that Angel of the
Divine Presence mentioned in Exodus, c. xiv.
v. 19.

Around Noah, and beneath him, are various
figures risen into the air. Among these are
three females, representing those who are
not of the dead, but of those found alive at the
Last Judgment. They appear to be innocently
gay and thoughtless, not being among the
condemned, because ignorant of crime in the
midst of a corrupted age. The Virgin Mary
was of this class. A mother meets her
numerous family in the arms of their father :
these are representations of the Greek learned
and wise, as also of those of other nations,
such as Egypt and Babylon, in which were
multitudes who shall meet the Lord coming
in the clouds.

The children of Abraham, or Hebrew
Church, are represented as a stream of
figures, on which are seen stars, somewhat
like the Milky Way. They ascend from the
earth, where figures kneel, embracing above
the graves, and representing religion or civilised life, such as it is in the Christian Church,
which is the offspring of the Hebrew. Just
above the graves, and above the spot, where
the infants creep out of the ground, stand two
—a man and woman : these are the primi-
tive Christians. The two figures in purifying

flames, by the side of the Dragon's cavern, represent the latter state of the Church, when on the verge of perdition, yet protected by a flaming sword. Multitudes are seen ascending from the green fields of the blessed, in which a Gothic church is representative of true art (called "Gothic" in all ages, by those who follow the fashion, as that is called which is without shape or fashion). By the right hand of Noah, a woman with children represents the state called Laban the Syrian: it is the remains of civilisation in the state from whence Adam was taken. Also, on the right hand of Noah, a female descends to meet her lover or husband, representative of that love called friendship, which looks for no other heaven than the beloved, and in him sees all reflected as in a glass of eternal diamond.

On the right hand of these rise the diffident and humble, and on their left a solitary woman with her infant. These are caught up by three aged men, who appear as suddenly emerging from the blue sky for their help. These three aged men represent divine providence, as opposed to and distinct from divine vengeance, represented by three aged men, on the side of the picture among the wicked, with scourges of fire.

If the spectator could enter into these

images in his imagination, approaching them on the fiery chariot of his contemplative thought; if he could enter into Noah's rainbow, could make **a** friend and companion of one of these images of wonder, which always entreat **him to** leave mortal things (as he must know), then would he arise from **the grave,** then would he meet his Lord in the air, and then he would be happy. General knowledge is remote knowledge: **it** is in particulars that wisdom exists, and happiness too. Both in art and in life general masses **are as** much art as a pasteboard man is human. Every man has eyes, nose, and mouth; this every idiot knows; but he who enters into and discriminates most minutely the manners and intentions, the characters in all their branches, is the alone wise or sensible man; and on this discrimination all art is founded. I entreat, then, that the spectator will attend to the hands and feet; to the lineaments of the countenance: they are all descriptive **of** character, **and not a** line is drawn without intention, and that most discriminate and particular. As poetry admits not a letter that is insignificant, so painting admits not a grain of sand, or a blade of grass insignificant—much less an insignificant **blur** or mark.

Above the head of Noah is Seth. This

state, called Seth, is male and female, in a higher state of happiness than Noah, being nearer the state of innocence. Beneath the feet of Seth two figures represent the two seasons of Spring and Autumn, while, beneath the feet of Noah, four seasons represent the changed state made by the Flood.

By the side of Seth is Elijah: he comprehends all the prophetic characters. He is seen on his fiery chariot, bowing before the throne of the Saviour. In like manner the figures of Seth and his wife comprehend the Fathers before the Flood, and their generations: when seen remote they appear as one man. A little below Seth, on his right, are two figures, a male and a female, with numerous children. These represent those who were not in the line of the Church, and yet were saved from among the antediluvians who perished. Beneath Seth and these, a female figure represents the solitary state of those who, previous to the Flood, walked with God.

All these rise towards the opening cloud before the throne, led onward by triumphant groups of infants. Between Seth and Elijah three female figures, crowned with garlands, represent Learning and Science, which accompanied Adam out of Eden.

The cloud that opens, rolling apart from

before the throne, and before the new heaven
and the new earth, is composed of various
groups of figures, particularly the four living
creatures mentioned in the Revelation as
surrounding the throne. These I suppose to
have the chief agency in removing the old
heaven and the old earth, to make way for
the new heaven and the new earth, to descend from the throne of God and of the
Lamb. That living creature on the left of
the throne gives to the seven Angels the
seven vials of the wrath of God, with which
they, hovering over the deeps beneath, pour
out upon the wicked their plagues. The
other living creatures are descending with a
shout, and with the sound of the trumpet,
and directing the combat in the upper elements. In the two corners of the picture,
on the left hand, Apollyon is foiled before
the sword of Michael ; and, on the right, the
two witnesses are subduing their enemies.

On the cloud are opened the books of
remembrance **of** life and of death : before
that of life, on the right, some figures bow in
lamentation ; before that of death, on the
left, the Pharisees are pleading their own
righteousness. The one shines with beams
of light, the other utters lightnings and
tempests.

A Last Judgment is necessary because fools

flourish. Nations flourish under wise rulers, and are depressed under foolish rulers; it is the same with individuals as with nations. Works of art can only be produced to perfection where the man is either in affluence, or is above the care of it. Poverty is the fool's rod, which is at last turned on his own back. That is a Last Judgment, when men of real art govern, and pretenders fall. Some people, and not a few artists, have asserted that the painter of this picture would not have done so well if he had been properly encouraged. Let those who think so reflect on the state of nations under poverty, and their incapability of art. Though art is above either, the argument is better for affluence than poverty; and, though he would not have been a greater artist, yet he would have produced greater works of art, in proportion to his means. A Last Judgment is not for the purpose of making bad men better, but for the purpose of hindering them from oppressing the good.

Around the throne heaven is opened, and the nature of eternal things displayed, all springing from the Divine Humanity. All beams from Him : He is the bread and the wine ; He is the water of life. Accordingly, on each side of the opening heaven appears an Apostle: that on the right represents

Baptism; that on the left the Lord's Supper.

All life consists of these two : throwing off error and knaves from our company continually, and receiving truth and wise men into our company continually. He who is out of the Church and opposes it is no less an agent of religion than he who is in it : to be an error, and to be cast out, is part of God's design. No man can embrace true art till he has explored and cast out false art (such is the nature of mortal things) ; or he will be himself cast out by those who have already embraced true art. Thus, my picture is a history of art and science, the foundation of society, which is humanity itself. What are all the gifts of the Spirit but mental gifts? Whenever any individual rejects error and embraces truth, a Last Judgment passes upon that individual.

Over the head of the Saviour and Redeemer, the Holy Spirit, like a dove, is surrounded by a blue heaven, in which are the two cherubim that bowed over the ark ; for here the temple is open in heaven, and the ark of the covenant is a dove of peace. The curtains are drawn apart, Christ having rent the veil; the candlestick and the table of shew-bread appear on each side ; a glorification of angels with harps surrounds the dove.

The Temple stands on the mount of God.
From it flows on each side a river of life, on
whose banks grows the Tree of Life, among
whose branches temples and pinnacles, tents
and pavilions, gardens and groves, display
Paradise, with its inhabitants walking up
and down, in conversation concerning mental
delights.   Here they are no longer talking
of what is good and evil, or of what is right
or wrong, and puzzling themselves in Satan's
labyrinth; but are conversing with eternal
realities, as they exist in the human imagination.

We are in a world of generation and death,
and this world we must cast off if we would
be artists such as Raphael, Michael Angelo,
and the ancient sculptors.   If we do not
cast off this world, we shall be only Venetian
painters, who will be cast off and lost from
art.

Jesus is surrounded by beams of glory, in
which are seen all around Him infants ema-
nating from Him: these represent the eternal
births of intellect from the Divine Humanity.
A rainbow surrounds the throne and the
glory, in which youthful nuptials receive the
infants in their hands.   In eternity woman is
the emanation of man; she has no will of
her own; there is no such thing in eternity
as a female will.

On the side next Baptism are seen those
called in the Bible Nursing Fathers and
Nursing Mothers : they represent Education.
On the side next the Lord's Supper, the
Holy Family, consisting of Mary, Joseph,
John the Baptist, Zacharias, and Elizabeth,
receiving the bread and wine, among other
spirits of the Just made perfect. Beneath
these a cloud of women and children are
taken up, fleeing from the rolling cloud which
separates the wicked from the seats of bliss.
These represent those who, though willing,
were too weak to reject error without the
assistance and countenance of those already
in the truth : for a man can only reject error
by the advice of a friend, or by the immediate
inspiration of God. It is for this reason,
among many others, that I have put the
Lord's Supper on the left hand of the throne,
for it appears so at the Last Judgment for a
protection.

The painter hopes that his friends, Anytus,
Melitus, and Lycon will perceive that they
are not now in ancient Greece ; and, though
they can use the poison of calumny, the
English public will be convinced that such a
picture as this could never be painted by a
madman, or by one in a state of outrageous
manners : as these bad men both print and
publish by all means in their power. The

painter begs public protection, and all will be well.

Men are admitted into heaven, not because they have curbed and governed their passions, or have no passions, but because they have cultivated their understandings. The treasures of heaven are not negations of passion, but realities of intellect, from which all the passions emanate, uncurbed in their eternal glory. The fool shall not enter into heaven, let him be ever so holy : holiness is not the price of entrance into heaven. Those who are cast out are all those who, having no passions of their own, because no intellect, have spent their lives in curbing and governing other people's by the various arts of poverty, and cruelty of all kinds. The modern Church crucifies Christ with the head downwards. Woe, woe, woe, to you, hypocrites ! Even murder, which the Courts of Justice (more merciful than the Church) are whispered to allow, is not done in passion, but in cold-blooded design and intention.

Many suppose that before the Creation all was solitude and chaos. This is the most pernicious idea that can enter the mind, as it takes away all sublimity from the Bible, and limits all existence to creation and chaos— to the time and space fixed by the corporeal vegetative eye, and leaves the man who entertains such an idea the habitation of unbelieving demons. Eternity exists, and all things in eternity, independent of creation, which was an act of mercy. I have represented those who are in eternity by some in a cloud, within the rainbow that surrounds the throne. They merely appear as in a cloud, when anything of creation, redemption, or judgment is the subject of contemplation, though their whole contemplation is concerning these things. The reason they so appear is the humiliation of the reason and doubting selfhood, and the giving all up to inspiration. By this it will be seen that I do not consider either the just or the wicked to be in a supreme state, but to be, every one of them, states of the sleep which the soul may fall into in its deadly dreams of good and evil, when it leaves Paradise following the Serpent.

Many persons, such as Paine and Voltaire, with some of the ancient Greeks, say : " We will not converse concerning good and evil ; we will live in Paradise and Liberty." You may do so in spirit, but not in the mortal body, as you pretend, till after a Last Judgment. For in Paradise they have no corporeal and mortal body : *that* originated with the Fall and was called Death, and cannot be removed but by a Last Judgment. While we are in the world of mortality, we must suffer—the whole Creation groans to be delivered.

There will always be as many hypocrites born as honest men, and they will always have superior power in mortal things. **You** cannot have liberty in this world without what you call moral virtue, and you cannot have moral virtue without the subjection of that half of the human race who hate what you call moral virtue.

The nature of hatred and envy, and of all the mischiefs in the world, is here depicted. No one envies or hates one of his own party; even the devils love one another in their own **way.** They torment one another for other reasons than hate or envy: these are only employed against the just. Neither can Seth envy Noah, or Elijah envy Abraham; **but** they may both of them envy the success of Satan, or of Og, or of Moloch. The horse never envies the peacock, nor the sheep the goat; but they envy a rival in life and existence, whose ways and means exceed their own. **Let** him be of what class of animal he will, a dog will envy a cat who is pampered at the expense of his own comfort, as I have often seen.

The Bible never tells us that devils torment one another through envy; it is through this that they torment the just. But for what do

they torment one another? I answer: For
the coercive laws of hell, moral hypocrisy.
They torment a hypocrite when he is discovered—they punish a failure in the tor-
mentor who has suffered the subject of his
torture to escape. In Hell, all is self-righteousness; there is no such thing there as forgiveness of sin. He who does forgive sin is
crucified as an abettor of criminals, and he
who performs works of mercy, in any shape
whatever, is punished, and, if possible, destroyed
—not through envy, or hatred, or malice, but
through self-righteousness, that thinks it does
God service, which god is Satan. They do
not envy one another: they contemn or
despise one another. Forgiveness of sin is
only at the judgment-seat of Jesus the Saviour,
where the accuser is cast out, not because he
sins, but because he torments the just, and
makes them do what he condemns as sin,
and what he knows is opposite to their own
identity.

It is not because angels are holier than
men or devils, that makes them angels, but
because they do not expect holiness from one
another, but from God only.

The player is a liar when he says: "Angels
are happier than men, because they are
better." Angels are happier than men and
devils, because they are not always prying

R

after good and evil in one another, and eating
the tree of knowledge for **Satan's** gratification.

The Last Judgment is an overwhelming of
bad art and science.   Mental things are alone
real : what is called corporeal nobody knows
of; its dwelling-place is a fallacy, and its
existence an imposture.   Where is the existence out of mind, or thought ?—where is it but
in the mind of a fool.   Some people flatter
themselves that there will be no Last Judgment, and that bad art will be adopted and
mixed with good art—that error or experiment
will make a part of truth ; and they boast
that it is its foundation.   These people flatter
themselves ; I will not flatter them.   Error is
created, truth is eternal.   Error or creation
will be burned up, and then, and not till then,
truth or eternity will appear.   It is burned
up the moment men cease to behold it.   I
assert, for myself, that I do not behold the
outward creation, and that to me it is hindrance
and not action.   "What !" it will be ques-
tioned ; "when the sun rises, do you not see
a round disc of fire, somewhat like a guinea ?"
Oh ! no, no ! I see an innumerable company
of the heavenly host, crying : "Holy, holy,
holy is the Lord God Almighty !"   I question not my corporeal eye, any more than I
would question a window concerning a sight.
I look through it, and not with it.

The Last Judgment will be when all those are cast away who trouble religion with questioning concerning good and evil, or eating of the tree of those knowledges or reasonings which hinders the vision of God, turning all into a consuming fire. When imagination, art, and science, and all intellectual gifts, all the gifts of the Holy Ghost, are looked upon as of no use, and only contention remains to man ; then the Last Judgment begins, and its vision is seen by the eye of every one according to the situation he holds.

THE END.

Printed by BALLANTYNE, HANSON & CO.
Edinburgh and London.

www.ingramcontent.com/pod-product-compliance
Lightning Source LLC
Chambersburg PA
CBHW031952060726
47497CB00016B/1467